D0059725

"You're a good list[...]

He swallowed and she watched the way his throat moved. "I have two daughters, so it goes with the territory. I'm gonna head down to the house and finish up a few things. You can stay here and watch the snow some more. But from the living room window, okay?"

Marnie grinned and felt herself melt a little. She knew it was foolish. Knew she was setting herself up for a big fall. Men like Joss Culhane didn't spare glances, attention or anything else on ordinary women like herself. She was smart and successful in her field. She was a good teacher. A good daughter. A loyal friend. But as she watched him leave, Marnie wished she were sexy and flirtatious, because maybe that would mean she would hold his interest...even if it was just for a moment.

Which meant she was in for one hell of a disappointment.

It also meant she had to snap out of it and remember why she'd come to Cedar River in the first place. It was for her mom. Her family. Not for love or lust or anything like that.

* * *

THE CULHANES OF CEDAR RIVER

Dear Reader,

Welcome back to Cedar River, South Dakota!
And to my latest book for Harlequin Special Edition,
The Family She Didn't Expect. This is the sixth book in
my new series, The Culhanes of Cedar River, and I'm
so delighted to have the opportunity to share Joss and
Marnie's story with you.

I've always enjoyed opposites-attract stories—you
know, that couple who meet and immediately think
they're all wrong for one another. Of course, the reason
they think anything at all is that there is clearly some
connection—physical, cosmic or otherwise. Which is
exactly what happens when Joss Culhane rescues
Marnie Jackson from the side of the road during a
snowstorm. She's a successful and bookish history
professor from California with secrets of her own, and
he's a mechanic and widowed single dad who doesn't
have time to wonder why she gets under his skin.

But when destiny collides, they find themselves directly
in its path. And when Joss's delightful daughters
quickly decide they want Marnie to be their new
mother, denying the obvious connection they share
is futile. Of course, the road to their happily-ever-after
isn't quite that easy—but in the end they know they're
much stronger together than they are apart.

I hope you enjoy Joss and Marnie's story,
and I invite you back to South Dakota for my next
book in The Culhanes of Cedar River series. I love
hearing from readers and can be contacted at
helenlaceyauthor@gmail.com or via my website at
helenlacey.com or my Facebook page to talk about
horses, cowboys or how wonderful it is writing for
Harlequin Special Edition.

Happy reading!

Helen Lacey

The Family
She Didn't Expect

HELEN LACEY

HARLEQUIN
SPECIAL
EDITION

If you purchased this book without a cover you should be aware
that this book is stolen property. It was reported as "unsold and
destroyed" to the publisher, and neither the author nor the
publisher has received any payment for this "stripped book."

HARLEQUIN®
SPECIAL
EDITION™

Recycling programs
for this product may
not exist in your area.

ISBN-13: 978-1-335-40808-2

The Family She Didn't Expect

Copyright © 2021 by Helen Lacey

All rights reserved. No part of this book may be used or reproduced in
any manner whatsoever without written permission except in the case of
brief quotations embodied in critical articles and reviews.

This is a work of fiction. Names, characters, places and incidents
are either the product of the author's imagination or are used fictitiously.
Any resemblance to actual persons, living or dead, businesses,
companies, events or locales is entirely coincidental.

This edition published by arrangement with Harlequin Books S.A.

For questions and comments about the quality of this book,
please contact us at CustomerService@Harlequin.com.

Harlequin Enterprises ULC
22 Adelaide St. West, 40th Floor
Toronto, Ontario M5H 4E3, Canada
www.Harlequin.com

Printed in U.S.A.

Helen Lacey grew up reading *Black Beauty* and *Little House on the Prairie*. These childhood classics inspired her to write her first book when she was seven, a story about a girl and her horse. She loves writing for Harlequin Special Edition, where she can create strong heroes with soft hearts and heroines with gumption who get their happily-ever-afters. For more about Helen, visit her website, helenlacey.com.

Books by Helen Lacey

Harlequin Special Edition

The Culhanes of Cedar River

The Night That Changed Everything
The Secret Between Them
The Nanny's Family Wish
The Soldier's Secret Son
When You Least Expect It

The Cedar River Cowboys

Three Reasons to Wed
Lucy & the Lieutenant
The Cowgirl's Forever Family
Married to the Mom-to-Be
The Rancher's Unexpected Family
A Kiss, a Dance & a Diamond
The Secret Son's Homecoming

The Fortunes of Texas: The Hotel Fortune

Their Second-Time Valentine

The Fortunes of Texas: The Lost Fortunes

Her Secret Texas Valentine

Visit the Author Profile page
at Harlequin.com for more titles.

For my BFF, Louise Cusack

I'm so glad I have you in my life.

Chapter One

Joss Culhane had planned to spend his Friday evening at home, watching a game on television, after
making tacos and hanging out with his daughters.
But at eight o'clock he got a message from his auto
shop's twenty-four-hour service, informing him that
a car needed a tow out on Route 14, at the base of
Kegg's Mountain.

He called the sitter, Mrs. Floyd, a woman who
had been watching the girls for him for a number of
years, and asked if she could come by the house for
an hour or two. Although the nearly thirteen-year-old
Sissy and ten-year-old Clare were responsible girls,
he wasn't quite ready to leave them home alone at

night. Mrs. Floyd lived only a few houses away and took about ten minutes to arrive.

"Thank you for doing this," Joss said to the older woman as he grabbed his coat.

"Of course," she said and smiled. "I'm always happy to help."

"I don't know what we'd do without you," he said and looked at his daughters. "Behave yourselves for Mrs. Floyd, I'll be back soon."

"Promise?"

He gazed at his older daughter, a hint of concern in the back of his mind. Sissy always made him promise he'd return, as though she feared his sudden disappearance. "I promise." He thanked Mrs. Floyd again, repeated his assurance to his daughters he would be back soon, and headed out.

The weather had turned bad that week, with snow falling intermittently for two days—common for South Dakota in January—but not welcome when he was called out in it. He drove through town, passing a snowplow and stopping briefly at the only set of traffic lights on Main Street to give way to a group of twentysomethings clearly heading for Rusty's Tavern.

Joss had lived in Cedar River all his life. The small town at the foot of the Black Hills had once been a vibrant mining community. Now it was more of a tourist destination or a brief stop for commuters heading for the state line. With just over three thousand residents, Cedar River was a good town with good people, and he was content to raise his daughters in the only place he'd ever called home.

He slowed down outside the famous O'Sullivan's. The hotel's parking lot was full, and the place looked busier than usual. There was a convention in town and he made a mental note to stay clear of the busy streets for the next few days. He had plenty of things that needed doing around the house *and* at the rental property he owned down the street from his own place. The house was getting a new tenant the following Wednesday; the painters had been in the place for the last two days and the plumber was scheduled for Tuesday to finish installing some pipes and tapeware in the bathroom. Plus, since the weather was so bad, he'd decided to keep the girls home for the weekend and not send them for their usual fortnightly visit to Rapid City to spend time with their grandparents. *His in-laws.* Lara's parents.

They'd never really liked him—never thought he was good enough for their only daughter. They were probably right, he figured. But at sixteen, he and Lara hadn't cared what anyone else thought. They'd been in love and planning their life together—which had included them both heading to college in Boise and getting an apartment together. But two weeks before their high school graduation, they'd found out Lara was pregnant. College was quickly off the table, Lara had got a job at a boutique in town and

Joss's Saturday-morning job at the local gas station had become a full-time gig while he trained as a mechanic to pay the bills.

Joss pushed the memory away and drove toward Kegg's Mountain. The snowfall was getting heavier and it took fifteen minutes to reach the site. He spotted two police cars pulled over on the side of the road. Recognizing his brother's SUV, he pulled in behind the other vehicle. An ambulance was in front of the police cars and he realized that it might be more than a simple tow. His brother's tall and broad silhouette came into view immediately as Joss grabbed the flashlight off the seat and got out of his truck. Henry "Hank" Culhane was younger than him by seven minutes, and as well as being his twin, was his closest friend. He was also the chief of police in Cedar River.

"Hey," Joss said and turned up his coat collar as the cold bit into his skin. "What's happening?"

Hank greeted him at the rear of his police SUV and pointed down the embankment. "Car skidded on the ice and swerved off the road."

"Anyone injured?" he asked, flicking on the flashlight and pointing the beam off the edge of the road, noticing that the small white sedan had come to an abrupt halt in front of a deep shrub thicket, landing down the steep embankment. Fortunately, the vehicle didn't look as though it had sustained any significant damage, and seemed to be at a reasonably easy and accessible angle for a tow.

"Nothing serious. Single-vehicle accident, only the driver in the car."

He gestured to the ambulance. "And that?"

"Just a precaution," Hank said as they moved further past the police vehicle. "The passerby who reported the incident said the driver hit the brakes hard. But I can't see any tire marks in all this snow."

Joss was about to respond when he heard a female voice speak loudly.

"I'm fine, please stop making such a big deal."

He heard a paramedic respond in an even tone about it simply being procedure, but the woman still resisted.

"Look, I appreciate your need to check me over. So, you've *checked* me over and you can clearly see that I'm okay. I just want to call a cab and find a hotel."

Joss flicked the flashlight downward and headed for the ambulance. He spotted a woman in a thin, shapeless black coat, standing beside two paramedics and a uniformed police officer, her hands flapping expressively in the air. She wore a red knitted hat, matching scarf, dark-framed glasses and gloves without fingers, and ridiculously high heels he knew were bound to send her tumbling on the slippery road at some point.

City girl.

No doubt about it.

He'd met a few of them over the years. And they weren't his type. Although Joss wasn't even sure he had a type anymore. Since Lara's death he kept his dating life simple—nothing serious. No commitment. No strings. No risk.

He saw the woman's arms gesticulate again and then she turned, facing him and his brother. Even though it was dark, there was enough light from the ambulance, his brother's patrol car and the flashlight in his hand to see her face. With her hat, glasses and scarf, all he could really see were her cold-reddened cheeks and mouth. She was average height, but the shapeless coat didn't give away any sense of her physique. Joss noticed the way her head was angled, and how her gaze flicked from him to his brother. He knew exactly what she was thinking. People always did a quick double take when they saw them together for the first time.

"Yeah," he said. "We're twins."

Although they were considered identical, Hank was broader in the shoulders and Joss leaner through the waist and hips. They had the same dark blond hair, but Hank sported a short crew and for years Joss had worn his hair longer and tied in a low ponytail. Recently, though, he'd cut it slightly shorter, even if it was still shaggier than his brother's. Joss also had several tattoos—whereas Hank was way too straitlaced for ink. And of course, there was the jagged scar that ran down his brother's left cheek, the legacy of a car accident when he was fourteen.

The accident that tore their family apart.

Joss shook off the ghost of memory and focused his attention on the situation at hand.

"Miss," Hank said in his usual polite tone, "my officer told me that your license and registration are in order, and your PBT came back with a zero reading."

"Just as I said it would," she said as she passed a quick glance to the young rookie cop now heading back to his patrol car. "Since you're obviously in charge here, can I go now?"

Her mouth moved motor-fast—like she was used to speaking a lot. It made Joss want to grin for some reason, but he bit back the action and waited for his brother to respond.

"Of course," Hank said. "As long as the EMTs give you the all clear." His brother turned to him. "Will you need me to stay and help with the tow?"

Joss shook his head. "Nah, looks pretty straightforward."

"Great," Hank said just as a message crackled through the walkie-talkie hitched to his belt. "Talk to you later. Take care of yourself, miss," his brother said and tilted his hat politely before he headed to his vehicle.

Joss ignored the staring woman and turned, quickly heading down the embankment. As he'd suspected, the small vehicle had turned on its descent and was at a reachable angle. By the time he hiked back up the embankment, the ambulance was gone, and so was his brother's SUV. The other patrol car was still parked with its lights flashing and the young police officer was standing on the edge of the road, talking on his cell.

And the woman in the shapeless coat was standing by his truck, hands on hips.

"So, what now?" she asked.

Joss hiked a thumb in the direction of her car. "I'll tow your vehicle back to my workshop and check it out in the morning."

She didn't look happy. "Is there a taxi service I can call to get into town?"

"Sure," Joss replied and then shrugged. "But I can give you a ride if you like, since I'll be heading that way anyway."

She glanced at his truck. "In that?"

"Or I can swing by my castle and grab the Maserati," he replied and looked at her. "It's up to you."

"Oh," she said, scowling a little. "You're really a comedian?"

"Sweetheart," he said with absolutely no affection as he opened the truck door, "I'm whatever I need to be. I just thought you might not want to wait for a cab in a snowstorm, but whatever makes you happy." He glanced down. "And you might want to stand aside while I get this done—don't want anything ruining those million-dollar shoes of yours."

She glanced down to her feet for a second and then stepped aside, still glaring at him, and moved around the rear of the truck, using the flashlight on her phone to guide her steps. Joss called out to the rookie cop still talking on his cell, told him to stand by the edge of the gravel, and then got into his truck. It took half an hour to get the car up from the embankment and hitched on the truck, and by the time he was done, Joss was all out of patience. For one, it had started snowing again, and for another, the woman with the unsuitable shoes was walking up and down along the edge of the road, her thin coat clearly not doing the job of protecting her from the elements. Typical city girl, he thought irritably, grabbing an oversize anorak from the truck.

"Here," he said as he approached her and noticed that she was shivering. "Put this on."

She looked at the jacket, then him, and snatched the coat without protest. "I've been trying to call a taxi, but the cell reception keeps cutting out."

"Yeah," he said. "Happens around here, and the weather isn't helping. I said I'd drop you in town. Unless you'd prefer to hitch a ride with the officer and sit in the back seat of the patrol car?"

Even in the dark, with only the flashlight and streetlight about thirty feet away, Joss could still make out her scowl as she dropped her bag and put on the anorak. "A ride would be great, Mr...?"

"Joss Culhane," he replied.

He could swear she sucked in a sharp breath, then figured he'd imagined it.

"Culhane?"

Joss's gaze narrowed. "That's right. And you are?"

"Marnie Jackson," she replied, thrusting out her hand.

Joss's gut took a steep dive when he instantly recognized her name. "You're the new teacher renting the house on Mustang Street?"

She stilled, her head tilting sideways. "Yes, I'm going to be teaching the fifth grade at the elementary school." Realization was dawning on her expression. "So, you're…"

"I own the house," he said flatly. "I'm your landlord."

Marnie Jackson had come to Cedar River for two reasons—one, to work as a teacher at the local school on a six-month contract. And two, to connect with her grandmother.

But Cedar River, South Dakota, was a long way from Bakersfield, California.

And she was a long way from everything she'd ever called home. From her family, her friends, the job she'd loved and worked hard for. But she'd promised her mother she would find Patience Reed. And she had. The older woman had married, had a family and was living her life in Cedar River—unaware that the daughter she'd given up over fifty years earlier had died, never knowing why she was put up for adoption.

Abandoned…that was how her mother had felt all her life. Why she'd never found peace. Why she'd never gotten along with her foster parents. And then her adoptive parents. And of course, why she'd given up on her own family and her husband without a fight. Marnie knew her dad had tried to make the marriage work, but in the end he'd walked out. He'd gotten married again, to a woman who had two kids, and lived his own life. Marnie still managed to have a relationship with him, but it was strained, with the shadow of her mother's problems hovering between them.

Now Marnie was in Cedar River, trying to reconnect the dots to her mother's family tree.

And the annoying man in front of her was part of that connection.

He was a Culhane. And Patience Reed's *other* granddaughter had married a Culhane. But not this one. Abby Reed-Perkins had married Jake Culhane—perhaps a cousin or brother of the man who'd towed her car and who was regarding her with obvious impatience. A man who was her new landlord.

Since she'd decided to move to Cedar River, the dots, it seemed, kept connecting organically.

Back in Bakersfield she'd hired a private detective to find out about her mother's family. And once she knew where Patience Reed lived, she'd planned her next steps and within weeks applied for the job at the school. It was a huge leap from her job as a college professor of history—but a necessary one if she was going to pull off a little subterfuge. She needed to go undercover for a while and what better camouflage than being a teacher at the local elementary school? Of course, she was way overqualified for the position, but she figured she'd be able to pull it off for a few months. She'd called the local Realtor a couple of weeks earlier, looking for a house to rent, and once she knew she had a place to live, accepted the teaching job.

The school principal had asked her straight out why she was applying for a position clearly below her usual status and salary, and Marnie had replied with an off-the-cuff comment about wanting to relocate to the Midwest for "family reasons," and left the explanation at that. Because really, it was the truth. What she wanted was to finish her mother's journey…to give her mom the closure she'd been denied. To find out why Patience Reed had given her up over half a century earlier.

And now, in town with a new job and facing the man who was going to be her landlord, she was neck-deep in her own deceit. Marnie inhaled, pushed back her shivering shoulders, raised her chin and met his gaze—no mean feat since he was well over six feet tall and she was barely five foot five. True, her shoes added some height, but the heels were digging into the ground, and standing straight was a challenge. Not that she'd let him see that, particularly after his sarcastic comment about her footwear. It was dark, but she had enough light to register the fact he was attractive and carried himself with a kind of loose-limbed, sexy self-assurance she would expect from a man with a very large truck and a bad attitude.

Seriously, girl, she thought, scolding herself for being such a cliché.

"You're five days early."

Marnie didn't miss the disapproval in his voice. "My plans changed, and I didn't get a chance to contact the Realtor."

"The house isn't ready," he said. "And probably won't be until Wednesday."

Her hopes sank. There had been a mix-up with the B and B where she'd reserved a room and she'd hoped the house might be available earlier. "Oh, well, I have no intention of causing any problems. Obviously I'll have to make other arrangements until the house is ready for me to move in."

His head tilted fractionally. "Let's get going."

He really was obnoxious, she thought as she trudged toward his truck, following in his footsteps and picking up the scent of some woodsy cologne that registered on some internal radar as adding to his picture of blatant masculinity. His hair was long-ish, she noticed, hanging below his Stetson. She bet herself a million bucks that he had tattoos covering bulging muscles, all hidden beneath the long coat he wore.

"My bags are in the trunk," she said a little more breathlessly than she would have liked. "I'll… I'll need them."

"Obviously. Get in the truck."

She ignored his terse tone, clutched her handbag tightly to her hip and opened the passenger door, noticing that the young police officer who'd helped get the car onto the tow truck was now driving off. The inside of the truck was messy and she grimaced as she hauled herself up. She held her bag in her lap once she'd buckled up and waited for him to start the engine.

"What were you doing on this road?" he asked. "You would have had to drive straight through town to get here."

Marnie sighed, her irritation rising. "I had a booking at a B and B a couple of miles from here."

"Had?"

She nodded. "Yes. But there was a mix-up apparently and the place was double-booked. Since mine was the second reservation, I missed out. So, what's the best hotel in town?" she asked as they began to drive off.

"O'Sullivan's," he replied. "But unless you have a reservation I think you'll be out of luck. There's a rock hound convention in town this weekend."

"Which probably explains the mix-up at the B and B," she said and sighed again.

"Probably," he repeated.

Marnie was sure he was smiling beneath his flat tone, as though he found her and the entire situation amusing. "Well, perhaps we can stop by the hotel so I can check anyway?"

"Sure," he said. "My time is yours."

She jerked her gaze sideways. "It is?"

"I get paid by the hour," he remarked. "Double time on the weekend. And since it's after nine o'clock on a Friday night, we're officially into weekend rates."

His words were drenched in sarcasm—and she knew immediately that he wasn't happy about being out on a Friday night. He probably had a family—a wife or significant other waiting for him at home. Whereas, she, on the other hand, didn't have anyone waiting for her.

Marnie tried to keep her voice friendly, but the man had a way of pushing her buttons. Perhaps him being her landlord wasn't such a great idea? "I'm sorry to be an inconvenience. Like I said, I hadn't planned on arriving until next week, but I thought it would be good to spend a few days in town getting to know the place before I settled in. I probably should have stayed another night in Wyoming, but I thought I had enough daylight left to make the trip, and then the weather turned bad and I got stuck behind this really slow RV and couldn't safely overtake for miles, and then I missed the Cedar River turnoff, and once it got dark I didn't have enough cell reception on my phone to follow the map, and the road was slippery and I—"

"Okay," he said, wincing as though the sound of her voice hurt his ears. "I get it, you apologize. Are you cold? I can turn the heat up."

She nodded. "Yes, thank you."

"You'll need a better coat for the winter."

She wondered if everything he said was a criticism, or whether she was simply cold and tired and feeling oversensitive. Whatever. Marnie held on to her temper. Normally, she was calm and controlled and measured in her response to things—a reaction she'd learned from an early age dealing with her parents' often volatile relationship. Once they had divorced, things settled down, but the cast had been set by then. Marnie was the peacemaker. Reliable and compassionate, a person who could be called upon to act as an envoy. Miss Dependable, her dad used to call her. The kind of person who could handle things.

But she didn't know if she could handle this.

She'd never ventured too far from California before. Never been too far from her extended family—her aunt Val and cousins, whom she had a close relationship with. Even her father, who she only spoke to every few weeks, had voiced his concern about her plans. But she had to keep her promise to her mother. For Marnie, it was about healing. To know that all the hard times hadn't been in vain. She'd loved her mom more than anyone, but she wasn't blind to how much loving her had cost. The memory of her mother's unpredictable highs, and then equally volatile lows, had left her yearning for inner peace and in a way, closure. And she hoped, with all her heart, that she'd find both of those things in Cedar River.

Marnie stayed silent as he drove into town, finding the loud hum of the engine oddly relaxing. He smelled good, too, she noticed once they were settled in the vehicle and on their way. Not of axle grease or anything like that, as she might have expected from a man who was so ruggedly attractive and blatantly masculine—but of that woodsy cologne she suspected lingered on his clothes. His wife probably picked it out, she thought idly, glancing at his left hand for a moment, but she didn't spot a ring. She turned her head to look out the window, noticing that it had started snowing again. The trip had been her first real experience with snow, and she'd had a harder time driving than she'd anticipated. Skidding on black ice, losing control of her car and plunging down the embankment was definitely a dramatic way to arrive at her destination. Thankfully, the vehicle didn't look as though it had sustained too much damage, and she was fully insured. It was inconvenient, more than anything, and she figured she'd just have to rent a car until hers was repaired.

And Mr. Grumpy Pants beside her looked like he could fix pretty much anything.

"So, you're a twin, huh?" she asked.

"That's right," he replied.

"Do you have any more siblings?"

He took a moment to reply. "Ah…yeah. Three other brothers and a sister."

"I'm an only child," she said, not having any idea why she was telling him. "I have a few cousins, but a large family sounds so wonderful. Sometimes I wish I—"

"Do you always talk so much?"

Marnie stilled. "I've been driving alone for nearly three days, just stopping to sleep at motels along the way… Sorry if I'm chattering on."

He made an indifferent, grunting sound and she figured he was all out of conversation. But she was interested. He was a Culhane—and since the private investigator had informed her that she had a cousin who had married a Culhane, it was a link, a starting point, a place to begin.

"So, you've lived in Cedar River all your life?" she asked.

"Yeah."

"When I applied for the teaching position I did a little research," she remarked, twisting the handle on her tote to allay her nerves. "It seems like a really lovely town. And when I was speaking with the school principal, Mrs. Santino, she said the town had a lot of interesting history and was something of a tourist attraction. Once I settle in, I'm looking forward to looking around and investigating the—"

"So, you do?" he asked, cutting her off.

"I do what?"

"Always talk a lot," he replied, glancing in her direction.

Marnie bit down on her lower lip. He really was a grumpy jerk. But since he was a Culhane *and* her landlord, she figured she needed to show restraint. Getting angry wasn't the answer. Instead, she stayed cheerful. "I guess I do," she replied.

He laughed and the sound rumbled through her like slow and distant thunder. She wondered if he knew he had the power to do that and then figured he looked so at ease in his own skin he could probably make her lady parts rumble, too!

Marnie pushed aside her foolish thoughts and looked directly ahead, into the blowing snow. She noticed he'd slowed the truck's speed down considerably. It was dark and there was no other traffic on the road as they headed toward town.

"This is Main Street," he said, speaking for the first time in minutes when they reached town and he slowed down again, slipping through the solitary set of traffic lights. "The hotel is just down the road."

"Thanks for doing this," she said. "I'm sure there

are plenty of other things you'd prefer to be doing on a Friday night."

"It's okay," he replied, not so much as a flinch in his stoic reply. "Here's the hotel," he said as he eased the truck into the driveway and pulled up outside.

Marnie looked toward the large building. The parking lot was full, and when she peered through the front doors, she noticed the foyer was busy. "So… can I get my bags?"

"You should probably call them first, or go in and check that you can get a room. I'll wait for you," he said flatly.

Marnie hesitated for a moment, then nodded and got out of the vehicle, trudging slowly toward the entrance of the hotel. Five minutes later she was trudging back out. As Joss had tried to warn her, the hotel was fully booked, with nothing available until after the weekend, when the convention would be over. The clerk behind the counter had given her the numbers of two other bed-and-breakfasts in town and she'd called them both from the foyer—but they, too, were fully booked through the weekend. She'd booked a room for Tuesday night and then headed back outside to Joss Culhane and his truck.

She opened the truck door and spoke. "You were right…the place is booked out until Tuesday." She quickly explained about the two bed-and-breakfasts. "Are there any other places in town you can think of?"

He didn't look happy and jerked his thumb backward. "There's a smaller motel on the way into town. You could try there."

"Do you know the number?"

He sighed and grabbed his cell and made a call. "It's busy," he said, disconnecting. "Sometimes the land lines get affected by bad weather. We can drive by if you want."

She nodded. "Well, if that's okay with you?"

He shrugged. "Come on, get out of the cold."

Marnie was back in the truck in seconds and they were pulling out from the parking lot. "It's a beautiful hotel," she remarked, clutching her tote to avoid shivering. "No wonder it's so popular."

"Yeah. It's quite the tourist attraction."

He didn't seem pleased by the fact and she wondered if he was grouchy about everything. They didn't speak again until they pulled up outside a small motel on the edge of town. It looked neat and tidy, but there was a distinctive neon No Vacancy sign flickering out the front.

"Right," she said with a sigh. "Unless you know of another motel in the area, it looks like I'm sleeping in my car or—"

Her words were cut off by the loud peal of his cell phone and he quickly took the call. "Okay, honey, slow down," he said after a voice spoke quickly on the other end of the call. "How about you go next door and see if Lucy is there?" He stopped and listened. "Okay, no worries, I'll be there soon. Just stay calm and wait for me," he added and then ended the call.

"Is everything okay?" Marnie asked.

"I have to get home," he replied. "The babysitter fell."

Her expression narrowed with concern. "That was your wife?"

"Daughter," he said. "Your search for a room will have to wait."

"Of course," she said quickly. "If you want to drop me off in town I'm sure I can—"

"Don't be ridiculous, I'm not going to drop you off on the side of the road," he said tersely. "Mustang Street isn't far from here."

Mustang Street? "I thought you said the house wasn't ready?"

"*I* live on Mustang Street, one house down from the rental property you leased."

So close? "Okay."

About four minutes later they were turning off from the main road and heading down a few smaller streets. She noticed the sign for Mustang Street, and when he wordlessly hitched a thumb in the direction of a one-story brick home, she figured that was the house she had leased. A few seconds later he pulled the truck alongside the sidewalk and switched off the engine. Marnie looked at the house. It was a large, neat one-story home with a blue SUV parked in the driveway.

"No point in sitting out here in the cold, so you may as well come inside," he said evenly as he opened the truck door.

Marnie shivered, nodding as she quickly followed him along the sidewalk and then through the gate and toward the house. The outside light flicked on immediately, and seconds later the door opened and a fraught-looking young girl stood on the porch.

"Dad!" The girl breathed out the word as though it was saving her life. "It wasn't my fault, honest. I didn't think that anyone would trip over the—"

"Don't worry, honey," he said, his voice so gentle Marnie's insides crunched up. So he wasn't 100 percent grouchy. Good to know.

The girl, who looked about twelve or thirteen, peered around him. "Who's this?"

Marnie took a couple of steps forward and managed a smile. "Hi, I'm—"

"Tell me what happened," he said, ignoring the question as he headed for the door, leaving it open long enough for Marnie to slip through behind him.

"I left my laptop bag on the floor and Mrs. Floyd tripped over it. Then I went next door like you said, but Lucy wasn't home, so I called you."

"You did the right thing," he said reassuringly. "I'm here now and everything will be fine."

The hallway was long and had a polished timber floor. There were photographs on the wall and a long coatrack and umbrella stand. Marnie hesitated for a moment and then followed behind the duo. Once she reached the living room she stalled in the doorway, noticing a sixtysomething woman sitting on a leather sofa, one leg propped up on a coffee table.

"It's not broken," the woman said the moment they appeared. "At least, I don't think so."

"How about we get you to the hospital," he replied as he moved around the sofa.

"Daddy?"

Another girl appeared, younger than the one who'd greeted them by the door. The two girls were now both looking at her, as was the older woman who sat on the couch.

"Hello," Marnie said and shrugged, figuring she must look like a mess in the shapeless coat, beanie, fingerless gloves and high heels.

He turned and she noticed he was still scowling. He seemed to do that a lot. "This is Miss Jackson. She's going to be renting the house down the street. And," he added as he gestured to the younger of the two girls, "apparently she's your new teacher."

Chapter Two

Joss had always considered himself an easygoing guy. He had a good circle of friends and was close to his siblings, ran a profitable business and owned several investment properties in town. Plus, he volunteered with the local emergency services, had done a stint on the PTA, gave a generous donation each year to the veterans' home and generally tried to be a good citizen—something he also tried to instill in his kids. People didn't usually get under his skin—but Marnie Jackson certainly did. He had no real idea why and didn't plan on wasting time wondering about it. Not when Mrs. Floyd clearly needed medical attention.

"I'll get you to the hospital," he said and looked toward his eldest daughter. "Sissy, get Mrs. Floyd's handbag and coat and grab the Ranger's keys, will you."

"I don't want to be a bother." The older woman sighed. "We could just wait for Lucy to get home."

Lucy Parker was a doctor and lived next door with her husband and young son. Joss figured she was on duty at the hospital.

"Of course, it's not a bother," he said gently, helping her to her feet. When she winced with pain, he realized she'd done significant damage to her ankle. "Or maybe we should call an ambulance?"

"Oh, no," Mrs. Floyd replied quickly. "I can manage to get into your truck. No ambulance, please."

He linked his arm across her shoulder and supported her as she hobbled across the room. They were halfway across the room when he remembered his passenger.

"I guess you'll have to come with us," he said, thinking it was the last thing he wanted.

She nodded vaguely and followed. Joss knew his daughters were curious about their visitor, but he wasn't in any sort of mood to offer any more explanations. He helped Mrs. Floyd to his truck and maneuvered her into the back seat, with both girls flanking her on either side. It left the front passenger seat vacant and within seconds she hopped in. Weird, he thought, how her very presence in the front

made him silently regard her as some kind of inter-
loper. Really, he was giving her way too much of
his thinking time. Maybe it was the way her perfume, or something, swirled around in the air and
lingered, and uncharacteristically rattled his senses.
It was flowery, like jasmine. Maybe it was lavender.
He couldn't be sure. He quickly put the thought out
of his head and got on with the job of driving to the
hospital.

It was Clare who broke the silence barely ten seconds later.

"Are you really gonna be my teacher?"

The woman beside him turned her head, glanced
at him for a microsecond and then looked toward the
rear seat. "Well, I am going to be teaching the fifth
grade at the Cedar River Elementary School. Are
you in the fifth grade?"

"Yes," Clare replied quickly. "Mrs. Corelli is usually my teacher, but she's having a baby. Have you
taught the fifth grade before?"

"No," she said and smiled, and Joss noticed she
had nice teeth. Truth be told, she had a nice-shaped
mouth, too. Not too wide, with full, pale pink lips.
She wore glasses, but even in the dimness of the vehicle he could see that her eyes were a clear blue,
with thick dark lashes. So, maybe she wasn't as ordinary as he'd first thought. "But I've taught college."

Joss didn't know much about her other than the
fact she was a college professor, wasn't married,

came from California and had excellent references. He'd left the details to the local Realtor who dealt with his other rental properties and wasn't interested in knowing anything other than if she'd be a responsible tenant and pay her rent on time.

Clare spoke again. "I had Miss Jeong last year, but she left when her boyfriend got a job at ESPN."

"What's ESPN?" she asked.

Joss waited a few seconds and then heard both his daughters and Mrs. Floyd start laughing. He joined in for a moment before he replied to her query.

"Cable sports channel."

She made a face. "I don't like sports much. I prefer to read."

"I like reading, too," Sissy said, and he glanced at his eldest child in the rear vision mirror.

Melissa—whose younger sister had years ago nicknamed her Sissy, a name that had stuck—was growing up so fast. Too fast, he sometimes thought. Soon, he imagined, he'd be dealing with boyfriends, the angst of picking out the right college and then the trauma—for him, anyway—of prom. She was a good student, quiet and studious, and showed an interest in going to medical school. But for now, Joss figured he just needed to get through the high school years.

He zoned out of the chatter, glancing every now and then at his daughters and the way Mrs. Floyd was putting on a brave face, and deliberately ignoring the scent of lavender or jasmine or whatever it was.

It took over ten minutes to get to the hospital and he pulled up in one of the parking spaces out front. It took another few minutes to get Mrs. Floyd into the ER. A nurse quickly approached and a wheelchair was provided. Joss ushered his daughters and *her* into the waiting area while the nurse took Mrs. Floyd into triage.

"Is Mrs. Floyd going to be okay, Daddy?" Clare, who was very attached to the older woman, asked.

"Of course she is, honey," he replied and ruffled her hair and pulled out a few dollar bills from his wallet. "Why don't you and your sister go and get something from the vending machine," he suggested. He waited until both girls were across the room before he spoke to the woman standing barely five feet from him, her arms tightly wrapped around herself, and wearing his coat. "Miss Jackson, I think you—"

"Doctor," she said, cutting him off.

Joss frowned. "What?"

"Actually, it's Dr. Jackson," she replied and then added, "I have a PhD in history."

Joss stared at her, still frowning, wondering if he looked as dense as he felt. "Huh? You want me to call you Dr. Jackson?"

"No," she said quickly. "I was only…" Her words trailed off and she shrugged. "Please, call me Marnie."

Joss didn't want to call her anything. "So, do you know anyone in town? Is there somewhere you can stay?"

She shook her head. "No. But I'll figure something out," she said and gestured toward his daughters and the sign toward triage. "You have enough going on without being saddled with my problems."

She was right, he did, but that didn't mean he was about to leave her stranded in a town where she didn't know anyone. "We'll sort something out, okay? Just… Look, I hate to ask, but can you stay here with the girls while I check on Mrs. Floyd? I'll be back as soon as I can, and I don't want to leave them here alone."

She looked a little surprised at his request, but her expression quickly softened. "Of course. Go ahead. They'll be fine with me, don't worry."

He nodded. "Thanks. I… Thank you."

Joss headed back to triage and managed to speak with the doctor on duty. Mrs. Floyd was going to be taken to X-ray, and although it didn't seem as though she had fractured her ankle, at the very least she had sustained a nasty sprain.

"You need to get the girls home," Mrs. Floyd insisted. "It's getting late and Sissy has to study for a math test on Monday."

He knew that. "I'll wait and drive you home."

She tutted and waved a hand. "Just call my son, Alec. You have his number. He'll pick me up. You heard the doctor—it's probably only a sprain, so nothing serious to worry about."

He didn't like the idea. "I think I should—"

"I insist," Mrs. Floyd said.

Joss knew the older woman could be stubborn about things—it was one of the reasons why she had been the perfect caregiver for his daughters. "Only if you're sure?"

"I'm positive," she replied and shooed him. "Go, I mean it."

Joss called Mrs. Floyd's son who lived in Deadwood and then returned to the waiting room. The girls were sitting together, opposite *her*, and chatting as though everything was situation normal.

"Yeah, our mom died," Sissy said, and he halted near the doorway as a familiar pain hit him directly in the center of the chest. "A long time ago. I remember her, though."

"I don't," Clare added and he heard the anguish in his daughter's words profoundly. "I mean, sometimes I *think* I remember her…but then the feeling goes away."

"I'm sorry about your mom," *she—Marnie—*said quietly. "I lost my own mom recently, so I can imagine how much you both must miss her."

"I really do." Sissy sighed. "She had brown hair and was really pretty."

"My mom was pretty, too," she said and smiled.

Joss saw his daughters nodding, heard the genuine compassion in Marnie Jackson's voice, and some of his irritation dissipated. Hell, he wasn't usually such an ass, but she'd caught him on a bad day. He was neck-deep in work at the shop, Sissy had been at him to go dress shopping and to get her navel pierced, and his in-laws wanted to see more of the girls.

Plus, Billie-Jack wants to reconnect.

Joss shook off the thought. He didn't want to think of his estranged father. He wanted to get his kids home.

She looked up and met his gaze and he managed a small smile. She returned the gesture and he looked at the floor and then thrust his hands in his jacket pockets.

"Ladies," he said and cleared his throat. "I've called Mrs. Floyd's son and he's on his way. It's getting late, so we should go home." He stopped speaking and looked at the woman standing beside his daughters. "And I guess you can—"

"Marnie can stay in my room, Dad," Sissy announced, cutting him off, speaking as though she'd made the decision and it was the most practical solution all round. "I'll sleep on the roll-out bed in your office, the one Uncle Grant uses whenever he's stayed over."

Grant was his younger brother. He used to live in Rapid City until a few months earlier and had often crashed at his place when he was visiting. Now he lived permanently in Cedar River with his new bride, Winona. They also had a baby on the way.

Joss got his thoughts back to the problem at hand—Marnie Jackson staying overnight in his house. It seemed like his daughters had the whole arrangement planned out. "Ah...sure," he said, discomfort climbing up his limbs.

"I couldn't possibly inconvenience you like that," she said quickly.

"Do you have another option?" he asked.

"No," she replied. "But I..."

"Then, it's settled," he said, not looking any happier about the idea than she was—but Joss didn't have an alternative to suggest, either. And it was only one night, right? And since she was going to be the tenant in his house down the road, anyway, it wasn't such a big deal. He could handle it.

"Thank you," she said quietly and hiked her tote onto her shoulder.

"No problem," he replied and shrugged.

It didn't take long before they were back in his truck. Joss ignored the way her perfume swirled around, and quickly concentrated on getting his daughters home. The drive back seemed to take forever, though, and he was stuck on the idea of a stranger staying in his house. Maybe he *should* take her out to his brother's place? Mitch and his wife, Tess, certainly had plenty of room in the big house on the Triple C Ranch. But it was close to eleven o'clock, the girls needed to get to sleep and he wasn't about to intrude on his brother so late at night. Tomorrow, he thought, he'd figure something else out.

He drove into the driveway and noticed how she

stared at her car on the back of his tow truck. "I'll take your car to the shop and get a look at the damage tomorrow," he assured her as they got out of the Ranger. "For now, I'll get your bags. Anything in particular you need?"

The girls were quickly out of the vehicle and heading for the house and Joss lingered by the back of the Ranger for a moment, waiting for her to respond. "There's an overnight bag in the back seat and the smaller of the two cases in the trunk. Thank you."

"No problem."

"I'm really sorry about this," she said and sighed heavily. "I can't believe there's nothing available in town tonight. I should have planned things much better and double-checked my reservation with the B and B. If I'd known, I might have been able to get a room at the hotel."

"I doubt it," Joss said and managed a grunt as he climbed up onto the truck, pulled her keys from his pocket and opened the car to retrieve her bags. "The convention has been planned for months," he added, and when he got down, she had her hand out for the bags.

"Well, I'm usually much more organized," she said, her hands still out.

"I got it," he said, tucking the smaller bag in the crook of his arm. The bigger of the bags weighed a ton and he figured she had more pairs of the million-dollar heels inside. Sissy had used her own key to get inside and Joss ushered his houseguest up the stairs.

"You know, I can use the roll-out bed. I don't want to put your daughter out of her bed and —"

"She's already offered," he said, cutting her off.

"Well, then, I'm happy enough to stay at the rental house," she said as they climbed the steps. "I'm moving in Wednesday anyway and I could pay an extra week's rent."

"Without plumbing and with the smell of fresh paint?" he queried and raised a brow. "Yeah, I'm sure you'd be really happy. As the landlord it's my responsibility to make sure you're taken care of."

"I can take care of myself."

Joss glanced at her car. "Yeah, sure looks like it."

Her mouth tightened around the edges and he thought she was going to offer some annoyed retort, but she didn't. She bit back whatever she wanted to say and then smiled extra sweetly, like the action made her churn inside but she wasn't going to let him see she was irritated by his sarcastic response.

"Look," he said and sighed. "It was an accident, I get it."

Once they were inside, Joss headed directly for Sissy's bedroom and dropped the bags at the foot of the bed. He turned on his heels and saw Marnie Jackson standing directly behind him, one hand on her hip, the other held up in midair.

"What's wrong?" he asked, seeing the query in her expression.

She sighed in exasperation. "Ah...nothing."

Joss's brows shot up. "Are you sure?"

She shrugged. "Well, it's just that you say you're okay with my being here, Mr. Culhane, but your body language kind of says otherwise."

Joss's brows shot up and he straightened his back. "My body language?"

Color leached up her neck and she waved an arm. "Well, you know, the way you...move and such."

The flush on her cheeks intensified and Joss bit back a grin. It had been a long time since he'd seen a woman blush up close. Plus, she wasn't as ordinary as he'd first thought. For one, she had incredibly blue eyes and her blondish brown, shoulder-length hair swished when she moved. With her chin set at a defiant angle and her eyes glaring at him through her glasses, Joss experienced a little jolt of awareness that he was completely unprepared for.

Not a chance, Culhane. Get a grip.

"Ah, you're watching me move?" he shot back.

"Well, no," she replied quickly. "I didn't mean it like I was *watching* you..." Her words trailed off and she threw up both hands with clear exasperation. "Forget I said anything. Just know that I appreciate your hospitality, Mr. Culhane."

"Sure," he said and shrugged, realizing he was being a jerk. "The bathroom is the second door on the right. The kitchen is down the hall and past the living room. Help yourself to whatever you want. I'll get the girls settled for the night. And, it's Joss."

"What?"

"My name, it's Joss."

He left the room quickly, ignoring the way her hair shone beneath the bedroom light, and the way his stomach was in knots. He wasn't the guy who got wound up by a pretty face. Hell, she wasn't even pretty, right?

Wrong.

Marnie stared at her bags for a few moments and then looked around the room. It was a typical girls' bedroom—not unlike the one she'd had when she'd spent time at her father's home as a teenager. Stuck to the walls were several posters of the latest pop idols, and she was amused to see a popular teen magazine on the desk that had a picture of her cousin Shay on the front. She hadn't seen her cousin for a while, but Shay Logan was one of the most successful country singers of the last decade and Marnie was very proud of her achievements.

Marnie glanced at her bags. She'd kill for a shower…but the idea of standing naked beneath the water spray while Joss Culhane was just fifty feet away made her rethink the idea. Not that she felt unsafe—she didn't. And his daughters were just down the hall. Plus, he didn't seem to like her one iota. But deep down she was cautious by nature and he was a stranger and she had no intention of being any more vulnerable than she needed to be.

She tucked her tote underneath the bed, grabbed her cell phone and headed down the hall.

The kitchen was large, with Western red cedar cupboards, Shaker-style cabinets and dark gray stone countertops. There were pots hanging from metal grids, and rows of spices on shelves near the large gas oven. Marnie loved to cook and the frustrated chef inside her felt the instant urge to start chopping, stirring and tasting. There were a couple of abstract paintings on one wall, a large oak table with matching chairs and pottery mugs hanging from hooks on a tall dresser.

"Everything okay?"

She jumped at the sound of a deep voice behind her and quickly swiveled on her heel. *Joss.* Boy, he was impressive to look at. Great shoulders. Strong arms. Glittering green eyes and thick, inky lashes. And a golden brownish blond head of hair that she'd bet would feel divine threaded between her fingertips.

Snap. Right. Out. Of. This.

"Ah…fine," she lied and swallowed the dryness in her throat.

"Coffee?" he asked and moved past her, leaving the scent of some subtle cologne lingering in his wake. Or maybe it was just laundry detergent off his clothes, or crazy male pheromones. Whatever it was, it struck her hard—like a frying pan over the head—and she realized she hadn't had a reaction like this to a man in a long time. The truth was, she'd been hibernating since her last failed relationship—declining offers to date, avoiding social invitations, holing herself away in her lonely apartment to lick her wounds in private.

Looking back, she should have had more sense than to get involved with another professor at college—particularly one who had a reputation for dating his students. But it was hard to deny what she wanted—and Marnie had wanted Heath. For a while it seemed as though he'd wanted her in return. They dated, attended family functions together, planned on moving in together—all the usual things. And then he cheated—once, twice, three times. Looking back, she should have bailed the first time it happened. But she'd forgiven him. She'd buckled under the pressure from her friends and taken him back. Until the last time. Her mother's death, finding Patience Reed—it had been exactly the lifeline she'd needed to get out of Dodge and avoid the pity from her friends and colleagues who knew exactly what Heath Sutton was like.

"So, yes? No?"

Marnie got her thoughts back onto the present. "Ah, sorry, what?"

"Coffee? Or tea?" he repeated, clearly bemused at her state of distraction.

"No, thank you," she replied and managed a step forward. "I'll never get to sleep if I have caffeine. Not that I'll probably sleep anyhow—I'm not good in strange beds and I—" She stopped midsentence and managed a brittle half laugh. "I'm doing it, right? Talking too much?" It was her go-to response, her way of keeping a lid on her nerves or anxiety.

He didn't reply, and instead opened the refrigerator to withdraw a bottle of water. "Here," he said, pushing the bottle across the benchtop.

She took the drink and stepped back. "How long ago did your wife pass away?" she said, taking a seat at the table.

He looked up, meeting her gaze, clearly not expecting the question. "Eight years ago."

"I'm sorry. She must have been so young."

"Twenty-three," he replied.

Marnie wanted to ask more questions. She wanted to know about his family. About his connection to her grandmother Patience, and her cousin Abby Culhane. But she stayed silent, sipping on the bottled water.

"So tell me, why have *you* come to Cedar River?"

His blunt question startled her, and her eyes widened instantly. "I...took a job here."

"One you're overqualified for, correct?"

She managed a shrug. "A little."

"You're from California?" he queried. "Teaching jobs in short supply there?"

"I wanted a change of pace," she fibbed.

"Well, you'll certainly get that in Cedar River."

"That was the plan," she said and shrugged lightly. "Well, I'm really tired, so I think I'll go to bed. Thank you again for your hospitality."

"No problem. I've left a fresh towel out for you in the bathroom."

"Oh, well I—"

"There's a lock on the door," he said, his gaze unwavering. "In case you were wondering. And you can jam a chair under the doorknob in the bedroom if you're worried."

"I'm not worried," she shot back quickly.

"Good," he said. "You don't have any reason to be."

Because I'm not interested in you in the slightest.

He didn't say it, of course. He didn't have to. The words were there, though, in the tone of his voice and the stiff-backed body language. Marnie had felt invisible to male attention in the past, but never quite so much as in that moment. She was relieved, of course. And put at ease.

And maybe, just maybe, a little bit hurt.

"Well, good night," she said and left the room without a backward glance.

She *did* take a shower, after locking the door because she could. She savored the lovely hot water and used her favorite shower soap before quickly drying off with the fluffy towel he'd provided. She slipped into fresh underwear and light sweats, and when she emerged from the bathroom the hall light was off and a lamp was on in the bedroom. She noticed a chair tucked discreetly by the door and lingered in the doorway for a second, listening to any sounds in the large house. She heard the faint hiss of a shower from the other end of the home and figured he must have an en suite bathroom. With all thoughts of him naked and showering pushed firmly from her head, Marnie closed herself into the bedroom. She didn't use the chair as a doorstop because she knew there was no need. After everything he'd done that night to help her try and resolve her lodging issues, she found it a little hard to believe he'd be making any moves. Especially with his daughters sleeping right in the next room. She popped her laundry into a spare bag, aired out her damp shoes and then slipped into bed.

And surprisingly, she did sleep. The bed was small but comfortable, and her many days of highway driving and motel rooms caught up with her. The result was that she didn't stir until nearly eight o'clock. She could hear sounds coming from other parts of the house and took a few seconds to assimilate herself to her surroundings as she fumbled to find her glasses on the small bedside table. Marnie took in the room in a quick glance and then swung her legs off the bed. She changed into black slacks, sensible flats and a bright red sweater, brushed her hair and made a quick bathroom stop before she followed the sound of voices coming from the kitchen.

She stilled in the doorway and watched the unfolding scene. Joss Culhane was standing by the stove flipping pancakes and his daughters were sitting on stools on the other side of the countertop, decorating the cooked pancakes with strawberries, icing sugar and maple syrup.

"Good morning," he said, his back to her, and Marnie wondered if he possessed some kind of sixth sense. "Are you hungry?"

"Daddy makes the worst pancakes in the world!" the younger of the girls announced and Marnie remembered that her name was Clare.

He swiveled his head around, offered a brief grin and then motioned to the spare stool. "Everyone's a critic. How'd you sleep?"

"Like a log," she replied and slid in between his daughters. "Must be all this clean country air."

He nodded. "Beats the city smog, I imagine."

"Yes," she replied. "But I come from a town called Bakersfield, which is small by some standards. It's certainly not like LA."

"Wait until summer," he said and pushed a coffee mug toward her. "The sky is so blue and the air so clear it defies belief."

"That's because cold air is denser and moves

slower than warm air. Which means it traps the pollution and doesn't move it away as fast as warm air."

He stared at her. "Ah—okay."

Marnie immediately felt like a complete geek and realized she must have sounded like a know-it-all, as well. "Sorry—occupational hazard."

"Weather reports?"

"Always having an answer to a question," she replied. "Although, in this case, it wasn't a question and I'm doing it again."

"Doing what?"

She made a face. "Talking too much."

"I'm not sure that's gonna change anytime soon," he said and returned his attention to the skillet. "There's milk in the fridge and sugar in the pantry if you need it for your coffee."

"I'm sweet enough," she said and then wished she hadn't because he was regarding her with a kind of amused disbelief and she felt heat rise up her neck once again.

"Are you?" he asked.

Marnie met his gaze over the top of her glasses with fake confidence. "Apparently."

Clare giggled. "I think I'm gonna like having you as my teacher, Miss Jackson."

Marnie smiled. "I think I'm going to like it, too."

"Daddy," Clare said in between a mouthful of pancake. "Are we going to the ranch today?"

"Not today," he replied. "There's more snow coming. Maybe tomorrow."

He passed her a plate with a short stack of pancakes and Sissy poured maple syrup over the top right before Clare dusted the plate with icing sugar.

She took a mouthful of rubbery pancake and grimaced slightly, winking toward Clare.

The young girl giggled. "Told you they were bad."

He looked at them both with a kind of pretend scowl that was so sexy she could barely manage to swallow her food.

"They're not so bad," she fibbed and took another bite.

"See," he said and glanced at both girls. "Not so bad, after all."

While she ate the world's worst pancakes, sipped her coffee and listened to Joss interact with his daughters, Marnie's gaze strayed over to him. In jeans, loafers and a long-sleeved black Henley T-shirt that did little to disguise his ridiculously perfect physique, and with that damned beautiful hair a little tousled, he was so attractive that her furtive glance quickly turned into an all-out, unchecked, blatant stare.

The kind that could get a grounded, independent girl from Bakersfield into all sorts of trouble!

Chapter Three

Joss hadn't had a woman in his house for eight years. At least, not one that wasn't a relative or a babysitter, or the mother or grandmother of one of his daughters' friends. And he certainly hadn't entertained one over breakfast.

He kept his dating life simple—no commitment, no promises and no sleepovers.

No problem.

Except, he suddenly *had* a problem and she was sitting in his kitchen, chatting to his daughters as though it were the most normal thing in the world. He'd had his fair share of hookups and one-night stands over the last few years. He was no saint, but he wasn't a player, either. He'd been a good husband, faithful to his wife. He'd been faithful to her memory in those first years after she died. Even after he began dating—if it could even be called that— he didn't lead anyone on, didn't make promises he couldn't keep.

And besides, the woman in front of him eating his pancakes wasn't his type. Still, now that he'd seen her out of the shapeless coat a couple of times, he could appreciate her curves, and the red sweater added color to her complexion. She also had nice eyes behind the glasses.

Joss met her eyes with his own and held her stare, and she quickly dropped her gaze. He saw the flush on her cheeks, though, and figured his instincts were right—she was checking him out.

"Okay, girls," he said and was forced to clear his throat. "Dishes in the sink when you're done. And you have two hours of internet time this morning."

The girls left the counter quickly, with Sissy rolling her eyes at him because he was the most uncool father in the universe and didn't understand that she needed at least six hours of social media time every day. But he had rules, and even though she didn't always agree, Sissy usually stuck to them.

"They're such lovely girls."

He looked at Marnie, who was still sitting at the counter. "I'm lucky."

"I don't know about that," she said and got to her

feet, grabbing the plate and mug. "Looks more like good parenting than luck."

Joss placed the skillet in the sink. "Thank you."

She moved around the counter. "No, thank *you*—for breakfast and letting me stay here last night. But I should get going and let you get on with your day."

Of course, he'd expected her to bail. Wanted it, really. Except for the fact that she had nowhere to go and they both knew it. "Ah—where do you plan on going?"

"Honestly? I don't know," she replied. "But I can't intrude on you any more than I already have. I'm sure I can rent a car for a few days and find a hotel, even if I have to stay in Rapid City."

"You could, certainly," he said and shrugged. "Or, maybe you can stay here and hang out with the girls while I go back into the workshop and check out your car."

"You want me to stay here with your kids?" she countered. "Without you?"

"Sure."

"Isn't that risky?" she asked. "I mean, I could be a serial killer."

Joss filled the sink with hot water. "Are you a serial killer?"

Her mouth flattened. "Well, no, but you can't know that."

"I know you're leasing a house that I own and have impeccable references," he said. "I know that you'll be Clare's new teacher next week. I'd say you're pretty low in the risk department, Marnie."

It was the first time he'd said her name. It was a nice name. Unusual. Soft. Womanly. Like she was. It suited her. She was close and her perfume swirled around, clinging to him for a few seconds and immediately shutting off the part of his brain that was determined to *not* find her attractive. Because that would be stupid. And he'd never considered himself to be a stupid sort of guy.

"Well, I suppose I could hang out for a while," she said quietly. "Until you get back. I'll try the hotel and the B and Bs around town again and see if any have had a cancellation."

"Sure," he said, nodding. "I'll probably be gone until after lunch, so help yourself to whatever you want."

She looked at the sink. "At least let me clean up the breakfast dishes."

Joss instantly took a step back. "Be my guest. I'll let the girls know I'm leaving." He asked for her number and she quickly obliged and within seconds they'd stored numbers into their cell phones. "I'll get Sissy to show you around and I'll be back later."

She nodded and Joss left the room, stupidly eager to get away from her and with no clue as to why. He'd called Mrs. Floyd earlier and spoken to the older woman for a few minutes, relieved to learn that she was on the mend. She would be staying with her son and daughter-in-law in Deadwood for a couple of weeks. It meant he'd have to cut short his working hours, but he'd do what he had to do. Joss headed for the living room and found his eldest daughter sitting on the couch, using her electronic tablet. He explained about their houseguest staying for a while longer and Sissy nodded agreeably.

"Dad," she said, "you know I don't need a baby-sitter anymore, right?"

"I know," he acknowledged. "Just humor me, okay? And Clare needs—"

"A mom," Sissy said bluntly, cutting him off. "Not a babysitter. And you know what—I'd kinda like one, too."

He sighed, hearing the lecture for the third time in recent weeks. Sissy had been at him for the past twelve months to get married again. And Joss knew why. Three of his brothers had gotten hitched in the last couple of years and Sissy was old enough to notice how happy they were. She adored each of her aunts. It wasn't hard to figure out that she and Clare wanted a woman permanently in their lives—all girls longed for a mother. But it wasn't that simple. For one, he'd loved Lara with all of his heart and wasn't sure he had room in it for anyone else. And two, if he did find someone, how could he be sure that she would be the mother his daughters longed for? What if he picked wrong? What if he allowed his libido to do the thinking and fell for someone who could possibly resent his kids? How could he be sure she would be the right…fit?

He couldn't. There was too much at stake. They were a family. A tight, unbreakable unit. Bringing someone else into that could potentially wreck everything they had…and he wasn't prepared to risk his family.

Joss clung to his patience, not about to get frustrated with his daughter for wanting a mother to call her own. "I hear you. Okay, honey? But it's not something that can be made to order."

"I know, Dad," Sissy said, sounding older than her years. "But it wouldn't hurt you to date, either. And I get it—you loved Mom a lot. But it's okay if you want to love someone else."

Joss's throat thickened and he swallowed hard. "Thanks, kiddo, but for right now I'm happy just being a dad to you and your sister."

"But what happens when Clare and I grow up and leave home?" she asked, her expression tightening a little. "You'll be alone."

"Well, fortunately for me that's a few years down the road," he replied, ignoring the way his insides twitched because his daughter was right. "But, I'll take your suggestion under advisement," he said and hugged her gently.

He left soon after and drove the tow truck back to his auto shop. It was still snowing lightly, and there were a couple of dozers on the roads leading into town, so the trip took longer than usual. Which gave him plenty of thinking time—about his life, his kids, his family. And his father.

Billie-Jack.

Joss still hadn't decided what he was going to do about his father. The old man had bailed when Joss was fourteen and had turned up again a couple of months ago—dying and hoping to reconnect with the family he'd discarded, before he passed away. Joss's younger brother Grant had apparently made peace with Billie-Jack, but the rest of his brothers weren't so easily swayed. And his baby sister, Ellie, wasn't exactly the forgiving type, so he figured she'd be the last one to make amends, along with Hank, who had more reason to hate their father than anyone.

Joss remembered the accident only too well. Billie-Jack had been driving drunk, with Grant in the back and Hank in the passenger seat. Inevitably, the vehicle had crashed, and while Billie-Jack and Grant had been thrown clear, Hank wasn't so lucky. Only the fact that Jake had been following on his motorbike and was quick enough to pull Hank from the wreck had saved his twin's life. But he was hurt badly. Along with the laceration to his face, he had burns to almost 30 percent of his body. Afterward, he'd spent years in and out of hospital, undergoing surgery and skin grafts. Billie-Jack was gone by then—having deserted his family in shame—

and Mitch, who was the oldest, had full custody of all of them.

He pushed the memories away and pulled into the auto shop a few minutes after nine and spent the following hour with one of his mechanics, Stuart, assessing the damage to Marnie's vehicle. It was mostly cosmetic, with the front lights on the driver's side smashed and some damage to the suspension and radiator. He wrote an accurate quote, made a copy and spent another hour working on a car that had been in the shop for the last week. He really needed to find another qualified mechanic to help out, given how busy they'd gotten, so once he was back in his office, he wrote himself a note for Monday to place an advertisement for the position. He had two full-time mechanics on the books and a schoolkid who came in two afternoons a week, but it still wasn't enough to keep him off the tools and in the office. He had a bookkeeper who worked every Tuesday morning to keep on top of invoicing and payroll, but Joss knew that to build the business even further he needed to spend time working *on* the business. Still, he'd come a long way in ten years. He owned his home outright, had three investment properties in town and money in the bank. Of course, he was a Culhane, but having his own legacy was important, and ranching had never been his thing. He could ride a horse as well as any of siblings and helped out at the ranch if he was needed, but after his family, cars were his great love.

He left the shop around twelve and headed for the supermarket to pick up a few things and spotted his brother Jake in the produce section, pushing a shopping cart, his young son at his side. Jake was the second eldest, a former soldier who now ran a high-tech security firm with a friend from Sacramento. He'd married Abby Perkins a year or so earlier. Jake had only discovered he had a child when he returned to town following an accident that had almost killed their older brother, Mitch. Yeah, Jake and Abby had a complicated history, but they seemed to have worked things out—and Jake was certainly making up for lost time as a father.

Joss had long suspected T.J. was his brother's child, but had kept his suspicions to himself. A bad move, he realized now, since it was likely Jake would have returned to Cedar River years before if he'd known he'd fathered a son with his former girlfriend. But the past couldn't be changed—Joss knew that better than most.

"Hey, Uncle Joss!" T.J. announced as he approached.

Joss shook Jake's hand. "How's things?"

"Good. Abby's working all afternoon and tonight, so we're going to make nachos for dinner and watch football," Jake said. "There's some convention on at the hotel this weekend."

Abby was the head chef at the O'Sullivan's Hotel. "Yeah, I heard," Joss remarked.

Jake nodded. "If you're not busy you can bring

the girls over, unless they're with your in-laws this weekend."

"No, I kept them home," he said and then explained about the weather, the callout he'd had the night before, Mrs. Floyd's accident and his houseguest.

"So, she's staying with you?" Jake asked, clearly keeping an eye on his young son who was now a couple of feet away and hovering by a stand stacked with candy apples.

"She *stayed* last night," he emphasized.

"And you said she's your new tenant?"

"Yeah," Joss replied. "But she got into town a few days earlier than she'd expected and had a mix-up with the B and B she'd booked into. And of course there's no room available at the hotel over the weekend."

"Is she staying tonight, too?"

"I don't know," he said and shrugged. "It's kind of an unusual situation. She's going to be Clare's teacher."

"So you said."

"Anyway, I should get—"

Jake grinned. "Is she pretty?"

Heat crawled uncharacteristically up his neck. "She's not *not* pretty. Which is beside the point. Thanks for the invite but I'll take a rain check."

"You could always ask Mitch and Tess to put her up in one of the cabins at the ranch," Jake suggested.

He was already regretting having said anything. "We'll see."

"Or if you're worried about having a *not not pretty* woman in your home and also not having a chaperone, she could come and stay with us," his brother said, his grin widening. "Abby will be home by eight."

"I'm not worried about—" He stopped, realizing that Jake was dissing him and then looked around to make sure T.J. wasn't in hearing distance. "You're an ass."

"I'm your big brother, that's my job. Anyway, if it gets too complicated the offer is there."

"The house she's leased will be ready in a couple of days," he said, almost to himself. "I can handle a couple of days. Besides, she's not my type."

"She's not?"

"No," he affirmed. "For one, she's a college professor. And she talks too much."

"A woman who talks," Jake teased. "Unbearable."

Joss expelled a sharp breath. "I meant that she's— ah, hell… I'm not gonna get out of this without sounding like a jerk, so I'm not saying anything more. Catch you later."

He high-fived T.J. and then quickly got on with the grocery shopping, ignoring the heat lingering around his jawline as he pushed the shopping cart and picked out the things he needed. By the time he got home it was past two o'clock.

And Marnie Jackson was curled up on the love seat on the porch, wrapped in a fluffy blanket, apparently fast asleep.

Marnie was caught in that place between dozing and sleep and having a lovely semi-dream. She was home, in her own bed, sleeping in late on the weekend, and she could hear someone mowing a lawn in the distance as the scent of fresh grass clung to the air. But it wasn't a dream. She couldn't actually hear the familiar sounds, catch the scents. And she wasn't at home. She was in Cedar River. She was endeavoring to tie up the loose ends of her mother's life.

"Are you trying to catch pneumonia?"

A deep voice thrust her quickly out of her drowse and she jackknifed up, grappling for the blanket she'd tucked around herself. She looked up and saw Joss standing on the top step, a couple of grocery bags in his hands. Snow stuck to his hair and boots and even with the grocery bags, in his jeans and sheepskin-lined coat, he looked wholly masculine.

"Pneumonia?"

"Sleeping outside is a sure way to get ill."

"Oh, I was only resting," she assured him. "And I've only been out here for about fifteen minutes, so not long enough to—"

"It's snowing, and cold," he remarked, cutting her off.

"I know," she said and sat up straight, noticing

a small red SUV parked behind the Ranger in the driveway. "But it looked so pretty out here I just wanted to sit for a while. Sissy gave me a blanket and since they're both in their rooms I thought I'd spend a little time outside getting acclimated to this weather."

"Getting a cold, more like," he said and gestured her to return inside. "I take it you haven't dealt with snow before?"

She shook her head and got to her feet. "Only on television. I'm used to dry weather, so this is a huge change for me."

"Yeah," he said and waited for her to walk inside before he crossed the threshold and closed the door, "and you shouldn't take any risks."

"I won't," she said. "But it looked too good to resist."

"I bet you won't be saying that once you've lived in Cedar River for a while."

"Are you always such a grouch?" she asked bluntly.

He stopped midstride and looked down at her, the lack of space in the hallway suddenly making it seem ridiculously intimate. His cheeks were flushed and it made his eyes greener, if that were possible. "I'm not a grouch."

Marnie raised one brow slowly. "Could have fooled me."

"Actually," he said quietly. "I've been told I'm charming."

She laughed loudly and headed for the kitchen,

figuring that was where he was going with the grocery bags. She folded the blanket and placed it on the back of a chair and watched as he unpacked the bags.

"Need some help?" she asked.

He shook his head, took a sheet of paper from his inside jacket pocket and passed it to her. "Your estimate," he explained. "The damage isn't as bad as it could have been, considering."

Marnie looked over the page and nodded. "Seems reasonable. Thank you for doing that so quickly. I'll contact my insurer and get things started. In the meantime, is there somewhere I can rent a car in town? I'll need a vehicle to get back and forth from school."

He reached into his other pocket, extracted a small set of keys and pushed them across the countertop. "The car I drove home is the courtesy vehicle I keep at the shop. You can use that until yours is back on the road."

Marnie was stunned. "I couldn't possibly."

"You say that a lot," he remarked. "You need a car—I have a spare. And like you said, you need to be able to get to work. I need to make sure you can pay your rent, after all."

Marnie's expression tightened. "I've already paid the security deposit and a month in advance, but can write you a check for the next three months right now if you like?"

"There's no need," he replied and casually put the

groceries away. Once he was done, he took off his jacket and hung the garment on a hook near the back door. "Did the girls have lunch while I was gone?"

She nodded. "Sissy made peanut butter and jelly sandwiches. They were pretty good."

He made a face and then half smiled. "Did Clare talk your ear off?"

"For a while," she replied. "But Sissy made her settle down with a book on her iPad after lunch. It sounded like she has reading to catch up on for school."

He nodded. "Thanks for watching them."

"I didn't do much."

"You didn't have to," he countered. "Sometimes just being in the room is enough when it comes to my kids. They like to do their own thing, but they like having company while they do it."

"Well, I was glad to help. But I guess I should be going."

"Did you find a hotel room?"

Marnie met his gaze. "Not in town. But there's a hotel in Rapid City that has a vacancy."

"That's a forty-five-minute drive," he remarked. "And…" He gestured to the snow falling again outside the window.

She shrugged. "I know, but it's—"

"I could have the house ready for you by Tuesday, maybe even Monday afternoon if I can get the plumber out sooner," he said, turning to her, hands on hips. The gesture broadened the width of his shoulders and made her giddy for a second.

Stupid girl.

"Oh, I didn't think—"

"I can work on the place tonight and tomorrow afternoon," he said, cutting her off, "if you hang out here and stay with the girls. I don't mind leaving them during the day for a few hours, but I never like leaving them in the evenings."

Did that mean she would stay another night? Or two? Or three? She didn't think that was such a great idea—not when she was quickly discovering that she was ridiculously vulnerable to his broad shoulders and green eyes. Not that he had given her a second look—or even a first look. But she didn't want to get busted ogling him again like she had been caught that morning over breakfast.

"I'll stay for a while," she agreed. "But I can still drive to Rapid City tonight."

"Again, not a great idea," he said. "You're not experienced at driving in this kind of weather. If you really aren't comfortable staying here, I can take you to my family's ranch—there's a guest cabin there that I'm pretty sure is vacant. Or, my brother Jake and his wife have a big house down by the river. I actually bumped into Jake at the supermarket this afternoon and he said you'd be welcome to stay there if you prefer."

Jake Culhane? Who was married to Abby, the

cousin she'd never met and who probably didn't know she existed? It was a chance to connect more of the dots. But it felt wrong, like she was manipulating things too quickly, even though she was jumping inside at the idea of meeting the other woman.

Marnie met his gaze. Yes, he was a little grouchy, and yes, he did seem to push the odd button or two when they had a conversation. But there was also something very *honest* about Joss Culhane that she couldn't ignore. He didn't make her feel threatened in any way. In fact, her reaction to him was quite the opposite.

"I'll stay here," she said quietly. "If you're sure you're okay with it. I mean, you and Sissy and Clare are the only people I know in town. And in a way, I am responsible for you not having a sitter."

"You are?"

"Well, if I hadn't driven my car off the road and you hadn't been called out to rescue me, Mrs. Floyd wouldn't have been here and wouldn't have sprained her ankle, right?"

"Absolutely."

Marnie heard the humor in his voice and managed a tight smile. "Thank you for rescuing me, by the way."

"All part of the job."

"I know," she said. "But I appreciate it. And thank you for being so accommodating." She hesitated. "I'm not used to having to rely on other people."

He crossed his arms. "So, you're an independent woman?"

"I try to be," she admitted. "I live alone, I change my own light bulbs, I swat my own spiders."

"No boyfriend?"

"An ex," she said. "Who I was well rid of."

"Is he the reason for the change of pace you said you wanted?"

Marnie inhaled and half shrugged. "Partly. I also wanted to find myself."

"Were you lost?" he asked quietly, and suddenly there didn't seem to be any other sounds in the room.

She looked at him and saw no humor or judgment in his expression. "A little. My mom died eight months ago and it changed the way I viewed things. Changed me, I guess you could say."

"And your father?" he asked.

"My parents divorced years ago, and my dad remarried," she replied. "I still see him, but I was always much closer to my mom, so it was devastating when she died."

"Losing someone you love does change you," he said quietly.

Marnie's throat tightened. Of course, he'd had firsthand experience. "I imagine you'd know that better than most."

He nodded. "Yeah. But it's true what they say about time—it helps us heal." His tone softened, ever so slightly.

"I hope so," she said, sighing. "Some days it's all I can think about. How much I miss her, I mean. Other days, I do whatever I can to stop myself from thinking about it."

Something in his gaze flickered. "That's grief. And perfectly natural."

She knew that, but she was surprised by how easily he'd picked up on it. "You're a good listener."

He swallowed and she watched the way his throat moved. "I have two daughters, so it goes with the territory. So, I'm gonna head down to the house and finish up a few things. You can stay here and watch the snow some more. But from the living room window, okay?"

Marnie grinned and felt herself melt a little. She knew it was foolish. Knew she was setting herself up for a big fall. Men like Joss Culhane didn't spare glances, attention or anything else on ordinary women like herself. She wasn't beautiful. She wasn't worldly. She wasn't sexy or flirtatious. She was essentially a geek to the core. Sure, she was smart and successful in her field. She was a good teacher. A good daughter. A loyal friend. But as she watched him leave, Marnie wished she *was* sexy and flirtatious, because maybe that would mean she would know how to hold his interest…even if it was just for a moment.

She also knew she had to snap out of it and focus on why she'd come to Cedar River in the first place.

It was for her mom. Her family. Not for romance or anything like that.

And not to lust after the sexiest man she'd ever met, either!

Chapter Four

Joss worked at the house through the afternoon, repairing hinges on several cupboards in the kitchen, finishing off the tiling in the bathroom, and tried to ignore the niggling voice at the back of his mind telling him his motives weren't only about getting the house ready for the new tenant. They were also about not spending any more time than necessary around Marnie Jackson.

Dr. Jackson, he corrected himself. Smart. Sassy. Successful. Independent.

Like he hoped his own girls would be, in fact, when they grew up.

The niggling voice wanted to add the word *attrac-*

tive to the mix, but Joss pushed the thought aside. He didn't want to get distracted by that kind of nonsense. He had too much going on in his life. Since discovering his father had resurfaced and wanted to reconnect, he knew he had a decision to make. The old man was sick—dying—and he wanted to make amends. But some things were too painful to forgive; and Joss had only bad memories from those years after his mother had died, when Billie-Jack had given up on being a parent and found his solace in booze. The truth was, Joss wasn't keen to have that kind of drama in his life. Losing Lara had switched off something inside him and made him extra protective of what he *did* have—like his children. And they didn't need to witness him having to deal with Billie-Jack *if* he decided to reconnect with his parent.

His cell rang and he quickly answered the call. It was Mitch.

"I hear you have a houseguest?"

Joss sucked in a breath. "Jake's been talking, has he?"

Mitch chuckled. "Maybe. He said you think she's pretty."

Joss scowled. "That's not what I—" He stopped talking and sighed again, certain his brother was laughing on the other end of the call. "I'm not saying anything else about it. Or her. Now, did you want something?"

Mitch laughed softly. "Just checking in to see if

the girls want to come out to the ranch tomorrow. Tess is planning a family lunch. If they're coming, tell Jake to pick them up because he's bringing T.J., too, and I'd like to get the lessons done early, weather permitting…but you could come by later. You in?"

"Sure," he replied and explained that he hadn't taken the girls to Rapid City for the weekend because the weather had looked to be turning worse. "I didn't want them to get stuck there and miss school."

"Everything okay with Lara's parents?" his brother asked.

"Yeah," Joss said. "They want to see more of them, but Sissy is at an age when she'd rather stay home and hang out with her friends. And you know I've never really been able to do anything right when it comes to Lara's folks."

"They're still grieving, I guess," Mitch said quietly. "Understandable."

Of course Joss knew his in-laws were trying to fill the void left by Lara's death—but he wasn't going to be railroaded into forcing the girls to spend more time with them, which included their recent demand that they spend two weeks with them over spring break.

"I imagine they will always grieve," Joss added. "Lara was their only child, so they've only got the girls now. I get it." He sighed.

"You're a good dad," Mitch assured him. "You're doing the best you can."

Joss was touched by his brother's words. Knowing Mitch had his back meant a lot. There were only four years between them, but his eldest brother had guided him through adolescence and had always been there for him. From his young marriage to Lara's death, Mitch had always been there to offer advice and support. "Thanks. See you tomorrow."

He ended the call and cleaned up the tiling equipment, locking the house before making his way home. When he opened the front door he heard voices coming from the kitchen and walked directly down the hallway.

"Daddy!" Clare exclaimed when she saw him. "We're making cupcakes."

They certainly were. With one of his daughters on either side of her, Marnie Jackson had one hand hovering with a spoon over a bowl, and the other hand pointing to the flour and sugar and other assorted ingredients on the counter. It was a scene that smacked of familiarity. A scene he'd imagined countless times over the years. A scene he knew his daughters longed for. And it triggered something inside him. Resentment, maybe? Which was stupid because Marnie had done nothing other than be kind to his daughters—at his own request, too. But resentment was what he felt, and mixed with that, Joss was feeling something else. Something…unbidden.

Awareness.

Attraction.

Which was stupid, because she wasn't his type at all. He didn't like bookish types. And he didn't like blondes. And he wasn't in the market to be distracted by anyone, either. Still, he liked curves. And she had the most amazing blue eyes. And he also liked her perfume and the way her hair swished when she walked.

Fine, maybe she wasn't *exactly* his type, but there was enough awareness to hike his interest up a notch or two. Or maybe a little more than that.

"Hey," he said, meeting Marnie's gaze.

"Hi, there," she replied, her cheeks flushing a little, and it made him grin just a bit.

"How did they swindle you into this?" he asked, moving around the countertop.

"No swindling required," she said and smiled. "I love baking. In fact, I love all cooking. But making cupcakes is one of my favorite things to do."

"Dad's really the worst cook ever," Sissy announced, throwing him under the bus without batting an eyelid.

"Ever?" Marnie remarked, still smiling. "Surely he's not that bad?"

"He always burns the toast," Clare chimed in before he could defend himself. "And remember the pancakes from this morning?" she reminded everyone and rolled her eyes.

"Hey, I thought we agreed they weren't that bad," he said teasingly.

"They tasted like rubber," Clare supplied.

Joss raised a brow and looked at Marnie again. "Is that true?"

She dipped her chin and shrugged one shoulder. "A little. But to be fair, I'm more of a toast and bagel kind of gal, so perhaps not the best judge."

Joss's gut did a stupid sort of roll and he shook himself a little, trying to get the flirty edge to the interaction out of his thoughts. He didn't want to be distracted by flirting, or cooking, or anything else. She wasn't his type—end of story. And he wasn't looking for anyone who *was* his type, either.

"So, rather than cook, I guess I should order pizza tonight," he suggested.

His daughters gave an approving *yay* and Marnie shrugged again. "I'm easy."

He was certain that she wasn't. In fact, he would bet his boots that Marnie Jackson was as complicated a woman as he'd ever find.

He nodded, willing that roll of his stomach to quit. "Well, I'll leave you all to your baking for a while."

"Okay, Dad," his daughters said in unison and he figured he wouldn't be missed if he disappeared and took a shower. Or in a puff of smoke, given how absorbed they were in Marnie and their baking activity.

Back in his bedroom, Joss glanced at the photo of Lara he kept on the bedside table. Taken a few months after their wedding day, she looked so lovely in the black-and-white shot, with her dark long hair a little windblown and her smile as captivating to him in that moment as it had been back when the picture had been taken. He'd loved her with all of his heart and knew she'd loved him in return. Those were long-ago days, but happy ones, and a familiar melancholy pitched in the center of his chest. He didn't like to dwell on all that he'd lost, but some days it was harder than others. Lara would have told him to snap out of it and get on with things—and he always did—but he held on to the memory for a moment longer, remembering the wife he'd loved and the blissful life they'd had together. Logically, he knew it was possible to feel that again, for someone else. But he didn't want to screw it up, either. It was risky—and Joss didn't risk much in life—and with two kids and a business to run, he couldn't afford to make a mess of things.

Unexpectedly, his thoughts strayed to his houseguest. The girls had looked so happy in the kitchen, laughing with a woman they barely knew...and clearly longing for female company. Mrs. Floyd helped when she could, as did his sister-in-law Tess and his sister, Ellie. But Joss knew it wasn't nearly enough. He worried that they were craving things he couldn't give them. Sure, he did the best he could and believed he was a good father, but there were times when being both a mom and a dad was hard work.

He brushed off the thought and headed for the shower. When he returned to the kitchen a while later he discovered Marnie was alone, clearing away dishes, a pile of cupcakes sitting on a plate on the countertop.

"Where are the girls?" he asked, remaining in the doorway for a second.

She looked up from her task. "Sissy said she had some homework to do and Clare wanted to finish the last chapter in the book she's reading."

Joss walked further into the room. "You know they said that to bail on doing the dishes, right?"

She grinned. "I figured."

"Want me to get them back so they can finish the chores?"

She shook her head and he was sure he could pick up the scent of her shampoo as her hair bounced around her shoulders. "It's okay. I don't mind. I'll just finish up here and go to my room."

Joss sat on a stool and rested his elbows on the counter. "You don't have to hide in there."

She met his gaze for a second and shrugged. "I know, but I feel like I've intruded enough already and—"

"You're not intruding," Joss said quickly and picked up a cupcake. "The girls like your company."

She looked at him. "That's not exactly what I mean."

Joss ate the cupcake in two bites and when he was finished spoke again. "I know. Look, the house will be ready in a couple of days. The plumber is coming Monday to finish off the pipe work and you can move in Tuesday. It's three nights, tops."

"If you're sure…"

"Positive," he replied. "I'll take you through the house in the morning, if you like, so you can work out what other furniture and things you might need. Unless you've got things on the way here."

"No," she said quickly. "Just me and whatever I have in my suitcases."

"You travel light."

She glanced his way again. "It's a short stay, just a six-month contract. I have an apartment in Bakersfield that I'll return to when this job is over."

"Have you done this before?" he asked, suddenly curious.

"This?"

"Move to a different state for a short-term teaching gig."

"No," she replied and then paused a moment longer before she continued. "But I needed to take a break from my life in California, and Cedar River seemed as good a place as any to regroup."

"Regroup," he echoed. "Or run away?"

"A little of both." She shrugged. "Like I said, I was seeing someone. A colleague at the college where I worked. And as it turns out, he was seeing other people."

"Sounds like you had a lucky escape."

"Well, hindsight is a good thing. At the time I thought my heart would be broken forever."

"Hearts heal, haven't you heard?" Joss said quietly.

"Spoken from experience?"

He nodded, surprised by where the conversation had gone, but oddly, not experiencing his usual discomfort when digging into his feelings. "Absolutely."

"Was your wife sick, or was it an accident?"

Joss swallowed. "Cancer. But it happened quickly. Which I suppose was a blessing…although, back then it didn't seem like it."

"I'm so sorry," she said quietly, head bowed a little. "I can't even imagine how hard that was for you all."

"It was devastating," he admitted. "Some days, it still is."

Oddly, Joss didn't want to take back his words or change the subject. There was something about Marnie's earnest compassion that touched him deep down. Usually, he closed up when talking about Lara to strangers. Of course, his family knew how much they had loved one another, and how broken he'd been when she'd passed away. How broken he still was, in many ways—like his inability to let himself really feel an emotional connection to another woman. He dated casually and it never lasted past a few weeks or so. In fact, he hadn't hooked up with anyone for well over six months.

"You and your wife—did you know each other long?"

He met Marnie's level gaze. "We went to school together," he explained when her brows rose a fraction. "We dated through junior and senior year. We'd planned on going to the same college, but..." His words trailed off.

"But?"

"Lara got pregnant." He shrugged. "So, instead we settled down and made our life together in Cedar River. It's weird, but getting married so young always felt like a blessing—like it meant we had more time together. As it turned out, we didn't have anywhere near enough time."

She sighed and offered a tiny smile. "You know, I think I envy you. I've never loved anyone like that. I'm not sure I'd know how."

Joss's insides contracted. "I'm sure you do... I think it's just allowing someone in."

"Yeah," she agreed. "There's the tricky part—that means trusting someone not to break your heart. And I'm all out of trust at the moment."

"Not all men cheat," he said quietly. "And if your ex did that to you, then he wasn't worth having, right?"

She nodded. "Of course, logically, I know that. But logic isn't always in line with the heart."

"True," he replied, feeling weirdly at ease. As though they'd been friends a long time and talking about things so insanely personal was just normal, everyday. Which it definitely wasn't. He cleared his throat. "Thanks for spending time with the girls today, by the way. They looked really happy when I got home."

"They're terrific," she said and smiled. "You should be so proud of them."

"I am, and thanks again. For the chat, too. I don't usually get to talk about Lara to another woman."

Her eyes widened a little. "Why not?"

Joss hesitated. "Ah…because I don't have female friends."

She gave him a curious look. "You don't?"

He shrugged, heat crawling up his neck. "That's bad, huh?"

She smiled a little. "I'm not sure I have any male friends, either," she admitted. "Work colleagues, of course, and acquaintances, but no real friends. So, I take it you're single at the moment?"

The heat returned. "Yep."

"I wouldn't think that someone who looks like you would stay single for long in a small town," she said as her smile broadened. "I mean…if you were looking."

Marnie couldn't quite believe the words were coming out of her mouth. She also couldn't believe she was having such a personal conversation with a man she hardly knew. A man who was pure temptation, with his green eyes and unbelievably broad shoulders.

"I'm not," he said quickly and got to his feet. "So, I should think about ordering the pizza. Any toppings I need to avoid?"

She shook her head. "No."

He nodded and left the room and she let out a long breath the moment he disappeared.

Sheesh, girl, could you be any more obvious?

Marnie covered the cupcakes with some plastic wrap, quickly finished tidying up and then hid out in her room for a while, and called her cousin Shay, who picked up on the fourth ring.

"So, how's it going?" her cousin asked.

Marnie quickly detailed the events of her arrival in Cedar River, including the car accident and her unexpected living arrangements. "So, yeah, it's been quite an eventful couple of days."

"And you're living with this guy and his kids?" Shay asked, her voice dropping an octave.

"Just for a couple of days." She quickly explained about the house she was leasing. "I'll be in my own place soon."

"I feel like I should come and visit to support you," Shay said. "Especially when you meet your grandmother for the first time."

Marnie's insides crunched up. Of all the friends she had, and all the family she loved, Shay was special. She was kind and considerate and always on hand to help others. But Marnie knew that as a successful singer, her cousin had a busy and complicated life.

"I'll be fine. And don't you have three more weeks of touring before you head back to the studio?"

"Yes," her cousin said. "But I'd drop all that in a heartbeat if you needed me."

Her heart warmed. "I promise to call *if* I need you. I'm just going to take things slowly and see what happens."

"And the hot single dad?"

Marnie's skin heated. "I didn't say he was hot."

"You didn't say he *wasn't* hot," Shay replied and laughed. "And I know you, cuz…you never comment if they're attractive. It's like you think they're out of your league, or something. Which is ridiculous because you are gorgeous and smart."

Shay was always her staunchest supporter. "Thanks. I'll call you in a few days once I've settled into the new house."

"Sure," her cousin replied. "And don't forget I'll be there if you need me."

Marnie ended the call, brushed her hair and left the room. The girls were in the living room with their father and she hovered in the doorway for a moment, unsure if she should intrude. Clare was sitting on the sofa, a book in her hands, while Sissy was curled up on the love seat by the window, doing something on her cell phone. Joss was perched on the edge of a chair, flicking though a small stack of papers on the coffee table at his knees. She looked around, noticing an array of pictures on the mantel, some of the girls in dance costumes or riding a pony. Others of them with Joss, and then a few that told a sad and poignant story of loss. A pretty young woman, holding a newborn in her arms, her expression one of pure and unadulterated joy. For a moment, Marnie wondered if she had ever experienced a moment like that. And when she realized she hadn't, a wave of envy rolled through her like water curling over sand.

I've reached a new low... I'm jealous of a dead woman.

She shook herself off, cleared her throat a little and headed into the room.

"Hey," he said in acknowledgment.

Marnie managed a tight smile, staying where she was, and his gaze quickly reverted back to the papers in front of him.

"You can sit next to me," Clare suggested with a grin. "I can tell you all about the kids in my class."

"No gossiping," Joss said, without looking up.

Clare chuckled. "Daddy hates gossip."

"Me, too," Marnie replied as she walked further into the room, thinking about how she'd been on the receiving end of way too much gossip back when Heath had cheated on her. "But you can tell me what you like most about school."

"I like art class," Clare replied. "And we're learning about France this term, and we're going to be learning some French words, too." Then she screwed up her face. "Or at least, we were with Mrs. Corelli. Can you speak French?"

"Actually," Marnie said, sitting down, "I can."

She wasn't going to add that she also spoke Spanish, German and Italian, for fear of sounding like some kind of bragging know-it-all. Languages were a passion, but she knew people were often put off by what might be considered her overachievement. Growing up, she'd always been at the top of her class, always asking her teachers for more work, more books, more learning to stimulate her mind.

And socially, she'd paid for her desire to learn more. She'd never been particularly popular in school or college, more at home in the library than at a party, she'd always been responsible and level-headed. She'd never been drunk or even tipsy. Never smoked. Never raged or partied hard. She always stayed in control. She had to, with the way things often were with her mother. Still, she never resented her mother for the way things were. Marnie knew her mom couldn't always control her behavior. She'd learned to have compassion from an early age, even when things were really bad.

"So," she said, shifting the subject from herself and pointing to the instrument sitting in the corner. "Who plays the piano?"

"Dad plays," Sissy replied, glancing up from her cell phone. "I can play a bit, but he's really good at it."

Marnie suspected Joss Culhane would be good at most things.

Snap out of it, woman!

"A man of many talents," she said.

He looked up and met her gaze. "Not too many."

"He's been playing since he was a kid," Sissy announced.

"I really wanted to play the drums," he remarked, shoving the papers into a folder. "My mom refused to buy me a drum kit back when I had dreams of joining the Foo Fighters." He grinned. "I got a piano instead."

Marnie smiled. "I pegged you more for a country and Western fan."

"I like most types of music," he replied. "And all in moderation. Except for disco…that's just an entire era we need to forget."

She laughed. "I *love* disco," she admitted.

He scowled and then grinned and seemed as though he was going to say something else, but the doorbell rang.

"Our pizza!" Clare announced and jumped to her feet.

Joss left the room and Sissy suggested they head for the kitchen. "We're not allowed to eat in here," she said, rolling her eyes.

Ten minutes later they were all settled around the

kitchen table, eating pizza and drinking sodas. The girls lasted about half an hour before Clare pleaded she was too full to even move and needed to lie down for a while, and Sissy headed off to take a shower.

"And again, they've got out of cleaning up," Joss remarked once Sissy left the room.

"If it's any consolation," Marnie remarked, "I wasn't keen on chores when I was their age. In fact, I'm not overly keen on them now. I do them, of course, because I'm a grown-up and as a grown-up I am forced to do things I know are good for me, but they still suck."

He laughed and the sound vibrated through her. "Yeah, that's the kicker, hey, with being an adult. We don't get to ditch the hard stuff as often as we could when we were kids."

"Some do," she said and dropped the crust onto her plate. "I have a cousin, Trent… He's a hopeless case. He surfs and lies around on the beach most days. Of course, the whole family adore him, too," she added and smiled again. "My dad calls him a lovable loafer."

Joss grinned and then asked more seriously, "Are you close to your dad?"

She shrugged. "I try to be. My mother never really forgave him for leaving. Sometimes it feels more strained than it should be. He tried to be a good father, too, in his way, but he's hard to get to know and I don't think we'll ever have one of those enviable father-daughter relationships…you know, like you have with your kids. I guess, since my mom passed away, we're trying to work out what kind of relationship we have."

"I don't think parents deliberately set out to hurt their kids," he said quietly, meeting her gaze with a kind of burning intensity that warmed her through to her bones. "If your dad pulled away from you, perhaps he did that because he felt guilty for not loving your mom enough to stay."

Marnie stilled, her chest tightening. "I don't think my therapist has ever explained that as well as you just did."

He didn't flinch at the word *therapist*, and it made her like him just that little bit more. She knew how judgmental people could be. Her mother had struggled with bipolar disorder for many years and Marnie had battled it with her. Seeing a therapist had helped, but the wounds from those times still ran deep.

"Well, my father bailed when I was fourteen, a couple of years after my mom died, and left us in the care of my eighteen-year-old brother…so I know a little about screwed-up parents. I made a commitment to try to do a better job raising my kids than my own father did."

"You succeeded," she said, coloring a little, conscious that something was stirring between them. She couldn't peg it, couldn't stop herself from thinking she was imagining it. "The girls are amazing."

And so are you...

Gawd, get a grip!

"Thank you," he said and pushed back in the seat. "I'm not sure I can take all the credit, though. They're both a lot like their mother, Clare particularly. And since Sissy is two weeks away from being officially a teenager, I'm sure I have some challenging times ahead."

"Teenage girls are the worst," Marnie said and chuckled.

"Thanks for the tip," he said and drank some soda. "Is that why you've chosen to teach in elementary school...steering clear of teens?"

"I wanted..." Her words trailed off. "I needed a change."

"Why do I get the sense of it being more than simply wanting to escape a cheating boyfriend?"

"Because it is," she replied, choosing her words. "I suppose you've always been one of those switched-on people who've never needed to escape anything?"

"I've been tempted over the years," he admitted. "Of course, with two kids and a business to run, the options are limited. I get one weekend a fortnight to myself," he explained. "When the girls go to Rapid City to stay with my in-laws."

A free pass for a weekend? Was that what he was saying? He could act like a single, carefree guy and do whatever he wanted. That was what guys did, right?

"Are you close to your in-laws?" she asked curiously.

"Not particularly." He shrugged. "They never thought I was good enough for Lara. Then again, I don't imagine I'll ever think anyone is ever good enough for my daughters."

"Do they have any other children?"

"No," he said. "Just Lara."

"So, they're still grieving, then," she said quietly. "Understandable, considering the circumstances."

"Are you sure that PhD isn't in psychology?" he asked, his mouth turned up in a way that was altogether too attractive.

Marnie's skin prickled and an uneasy and heavy thrum began to course through her veins. He really did have the sexy thing down pat. He was ridiculously attractive. He was probably the most attractive man she'd ever met. And despite her initial misgivings— Joss Culhane was also damned nice to talk to.

It should have sent her running for the hills, because finding him attractive—*liking him*—was a distraction she didn't need. But Marnie couldn't deny the intensely intimate connection she experienced when they talked and spent time together. Of course, it was completely one sided. She wasn't foolish enough to imagine he felt it, too.

Or was she?

Chapter Five

Marnie woke up around eight the following morning after spending a restless night in the narrow bed, having stared intermittently at the ceiling, the window and the posters on the walls. She'd bailed quickly on Joss the night before, once she realized she was spending *way* too much time thinking about how much she enjoyed hanging out with him. And how much she liked him.

But lack of sleep had made her groggy. She gathered up her clothes and made a beeline for the bathroom, splashing some much-needed water on her face before she brushed her teeth and hair and changed into dark slacks and an emerald green sweater she knew threw color into her cheeks. She slipped on her glasses and looked at herself in the mirror. She'd always thought she had a nice smile and expressive eyes. A real woman, Heath had often said. Not fake or enhanced by fancy clothes or cosmetic procedures. Her sole claim to vanity was getting highlights in her hair every couple of months. She'd never liked makeup that much and mostly wore sensible and comfortable clothes. She wasn't a risk-taker. She was a sensible, organized, well-respected history professor. She didn't do *hot* guys with tousled hair. And she was suddenly extra weary from thinking about it.

And of course, because that was the nature of things, she almost collided with Joss in the hallway.

"Good morning," he said easily, and she could have sworn his gaze lingered on her mouth for a moment, then decided she was imagining it. "Since you're up, do you want to come and see the house this morning?"

Marnie stilled in her tracks, trying to ignore how good he looked in jeans and a polo shirt. And she quickly noticed he had a tattoo reaching his elbow. *Gawd.* Ink made her knees weak. Especially the kind of Celtic chain that adorned his arm down to the elbow. She'd bet her boots that he had ink in other places, too.

"Ah, sure," she said. "I'll put my stuff away and be right with you."

"Have coffee and breakfast first," he suggested. "I promise that rubbery pancakes are off the menu this morning."

Marnie smiled and her belly did a foolish loop-de-loop, before she scurried off back to her bedroom and took a few minutes to gather her swiftly dwindling composure. The quicker she was out of Joss Culhane's home and set up in the house down the street, the better.

In the kitchen a few minutes later, she looked around and spotted only Joss behind the countertop. "Where are the girls?"

"My brother Jake picked them up about half an hour ago and took them to the family ranch," he explained, passing her a coffee mug. "My oldest brother has been giving them riding lessons, along with Jake's son, T.J. The snow has eased off this morning so they should get a couple of hours in the saddle."

"They like horses?"

"The name Culhane and horses go hand in hand," he said and grinned.

"So you're, like, all cowboys?"

"Part-time." He grinned again. "We usually all help out when Mitch needs a hand. To be honest, Mitch is the only real cowboy, along with my sister, Ellie. The rest of us just get to pretend occasionally. Mitch is teaching the girls and T.J. about horsemanship and the ranch, so they'll understand they're a part of the history of the place. The Triple C is one of the oldest ranches in the county."

"That's quite a legacy to be born into," she said, feeling a little sting of envy. "It must be nice to be able to trace your family back for so many generations."

He nodded. "Yes, it is. What about your family?"

Marnie inhaled sharply. "My dad's parents died before I was born. He has only one sister, and I have a couple of cousins on that side of the family. My mom was adopted and didn't have a great relationship with her parents. They had their own baby when my mom was thirteen—so she was pushed aside pretty quickly after that."

It sounded bad—but it was a truth that couldn't be whitewashed. And she probably shouldn't have said it, because she didn't want too many questions.

"But you said you were close to your mother, yes?"

She nodded. "Very much so. What about you?"

"My mom died when I was young," he said, so quietly she actually took a step closer. "She had a heart attack, which was unexpected. I think I told you how my father took off a couple of years later," he said and shrugged. "He couldn't handle it. My brother Mitch was eighteen and got full custody of the rest of us."

Marnie knew a little of what he was saying. She'd hired a private detective to find out about Patience

Reed, and of course there was some information about Abby Culhane's marriage and her husband's family. Marnie hadn't been that interested in it at the time. It was Patience she wanted to know about. But now that she'd met Joss, she *was* interested—probably too much.

"Well, we can't pick our parents…and I'm sure most people start out thinking they'll do right by their kids."

"For sure," he said, moving around the counter. "Help yourself to whatever you want for breakfast, then we'll head up to the house."

He left the room and Marnie remained where she was for a few moments, sipping her coffee and thinking that she'd talked more to Joss in thirty-six hours than she had to anyone else in months. Even when she talked to Shay, or her father, she skipped over what she was really feeling. It was what she'd always done—to protect her mother, to be the one who had it all together and took care of things.

She shook off the feeling and memory and drank her coffee, snacking on a cupcake, knowing it wasn't exactly a healthy breakfast, but she also knew she didn't want to go rummaging through cupboards in someone else's home. Joss returned about ten minutes later, rattling a set of keys.

"Ready?"

She nodded and followed, grabbing her coat on the way out. It *had* stopped snowing, like he'd said, but the ground was wet, and she glanced down at her heeled leather boots, thinking they weren't exactly designed for South Dakota weather. With her fuller than fashionable frame, clothes were sometimes challenging to get right, but shoes *always* fit. Joss had on hiking boots and he shrugged into a sheepskin-lined jacket as they walked outside. They were on the sidewalk when she lost her footing and slipped, jerking forward, reaching out for the first thing she could find—Joss's shoulder. And then, of course, she slipped again, and both her hands were planted directly onto his chest as he tried to steady her.

"You okay?" he asked, looking down into her upturned face, the cool air smacking her cheeks and making her breathless.

Marnie met his gaze, noticing how the intense green irises darkened a little, so close she could see the pulse beating in his jaw. Her fingers itched, suddenly, with the urge to touch him, to reach out and trace her fingertips along his cheek. She looked at his mouth, noticed his lips were parted a fraction and felt his cool breath on her forehead. Her libido did a wild and uncharacteristic leap. She'd never been *that* girl before—the one who experienced attraction with such powerful intensity. Everything about her life was moderate, calm, controlled. But Joss Culhane, with his broad shoulders, glittering green eyes and sinful mouth, made her body stand up and take notice.

"I'm…sorry," she said unsteadily and tried to regain her footing.

His strong hands wrapped around her arms and he held her straight, the seconds suddenly agonizingly long and drawn out. "Better now?"

She nodded, curling her toes inside her boots to regain her balance. It worked and she slowly lifted her hands from his chest, startled by the electricity tingling her palms. And appalled to think he knew exactly what was going on in her head.

"Yes," she insisted and straightened her back as he released her. "Thank you."

Thankfully, the house was only a short walk and he stopped by a white gate, swinging it back on its hinges. "Here we are."

Marnie walked through the gate and looked at the house. "It's lovely."

"It's all yours," he said and ushered her forward. "For the next six months anyway."

Marnie followed him up the path and climbed the three steps to the porch. "How long have you owned the place?" she asked.

"A few years now. It used to belong to Mrs. B's mother."

"Mrs. B?" she queried.

"She's the housekeeper at the Triple C. She's worked there for years. When her elderly mother went into a retirement place, I bought the house as a rental investment."

He opened the door and she followed him inside, down the hallway and into the front living room. It was a little different from the photos she'd seen online when she had first applied, brighter and airier than the pictures had shown. There were painters' sheets on the floor and covers over the furniture and Marnie wrinkled her nose a little and then sighed. "It's lovely."

"I'll spend some time here today to get the painting finished."

She nodded and moved around the room, spotting the huge fireplace. "How long since someone lived here?"

"About four months," he replied. "I had a married couple in here for about a year. They were both nurse practitioners at the hospital and left once their contract was up. I've kept it vacant since then to work on the renovations. Most of the plumbing has been replaced and the whole house needed painting. The two bedrooms are down here, and a utility room I've changed into an office," he said and gestured for her to follow him down another hallway. "The bathroom," he said, pointing toward her left, and then walked a little further. He stopped outside one of the bedrooms and shrugged. "I have no idea if the bed is comfortable, but it's clean and in good condition. If not, let me know. You're leasing the place furnished, so I'll buy a new mattress if you need one."

"I'm sure it will be fine," she said as she glanced at the clean and comfy-looking mattress. "I'll need to get some linen for the beds."

"No need," he said and pointed to the cupboard in the hallway. "My sister, Ellie, went shopping with the girls last week and stocked the linen closet. And the kitchen has pots and pans and a full set of dishes and all that stuff...but let me know if you're missing anything."

"You're a very obliging landlord," she said, meeting his gaze.

His green eyes shimmered. "I'm an obliging guy."

"And modest?"

He smiled and the action made her belly somersault. "I've been called a lot of things, but never that."

She laughed, and in the small confines of the hallway, with barely any space between them, Marnie was quickly reminded that he was the hottest guy on the planet and she was...what? Ordinary? A woman who had happily relied on her smarts, not her looks, most of her life, dating men who were educated but average-looking by fashionable standards. And she was okay with that. She was okay with herself. She was proud of herself, of her achievments, of knowing that substance trumped being the most beautiful woman in the room.

"What are you thinking?" he asked.

"I'm not sure I want you to know."

He chuckled softly. "Tell me."

Could she? Would Joss knowing her heart was beating madly when she was so close to him, make her vulnerable?

"I was thinking that you really are ridiculously attractive," she said and then wanted to snatch the comment back. "But you'd have to know that, right?"

His brow rose. "I would?"

"Beautiful people always *know* they're beautiful."

"That's quite a judgment."

She shrugged, feeling the air between them crackle. One-sided, of course. She wasn't deluded enough to think he was affected by their close proximity.

"Why don't you have a girlfriend?"

The question was out before she could stop herself.

His mouth curled a little at the edges. "Do you really want to know?"

"No." She shook her head. "Forget I asked. It's none of my business and completely inappropriate and I can't—"

"I haven't had a serious relationship since my wife died because I don't trust anyone to care about my kids as much as I do."

It was quite an admission to a question she had no right to ask. And it made perfect sense.

Except…she wasn't sure she believed him. "Or

maybe you're afraid that you'll lose what you have? Afraid to feel again?"

He looked stunned at her observation, but quickly recovered. "Maybe. But we're all a little driven by our emotions, don't you think? Why else would you stay with a man who repeatedly cheated on you?"

It was a good question. At the time she'd put it down to pressure from her peers and friends. While her friends and collegues were settling down, getting enagaged, getting married, having kids, Marnie had longed for a loving and commited relationship of her own. But now, staring up into Joss's face, meeting his gaze in a way that was so intense she could barely breathe, she wasn't so sure. Peer pressure suddenly seemed like a weak excuse. The truth was a harder pill to swallow and even harder to admit to. But she said it, anyway, "I think I believed it was all I deserved."

Joss couldn't move his feet. Marnie had his number. She had him pegged without even trying. If he had any sense, he'd move his feet and continue showing her the house and forget about the way her perfume attacked his senses, or the way her mouth moved when she spoke. Or the way her hips swayed with an easy, elegant grace when she moved. He'd forget everything about her that was toying with— no, tormenting—the foundations of his good sense.

"No one deserves to be treated like that," he said

quietly and forced his limbs to work, moving down the hallway and into the kitchen. "This room and the second bedroom still need painting," he said when she appeared beside him.

"It's great," she said and crossed her arms, pushing her chest up in a way that had him quickly looking away because he wasn't *that* guy. But be damned if there wasn't something about her that hiked his awareness up a notch or two. Or more. "I'm looking forward to moving in."

And Joss was looking forward to her moving *out*.

He didn't need any more distraction in the form of quiet, earnest conversations. Or smiles that made his gut churn. Or to have her perfume winding its way through him and attacking his libido.

"I'm going to head to the ranch midmorning to collect the girls. My sister-in-law is putting on a lunch thing for the family. You're welcome to come with me."

Please don't say yes...

She uncrossed her arms. "Ah...okay."

"You don't have to," he said quickly, backpedaling, because he really didn't want to spend any more time with her and then question his motives. He didn't like her, right? She was too irritating. She was too intuitive. Not his type. "If you'd rather stay—"

"I said I would go," she replied and moved further into the room.

That settled, they stayed for another few minutes

and then Joss locked up and they headed home. He disappeared into his study for a while, muttering something about having work to do, and emerged around ten thirty, finding her in the living room flicking through something on her cell phone.

"Ready to go?" he asked.

She nodded and got to her feet and minutes later they were on their way. The Triple C was on the other side of town and the drive took about twenty minutes. Enough time for Joss to stay quiet and convince himself that he wasn't, in any way whatsoever, attracted to Marnie Jackson.

Except, she kept talking. About the weather. About the snow. About how she planned on doing some sightseeing once her car was back on the road. About how much she was looking forward to settling into the house and starting work at the school. And he liked the sound of her voice—it was soft and a little husky, with a gentle lilt at the end of each word. It was oddly soothing and, for some reason he couldn't define, evoked a surge of memory, reminding him of things he'd long forgotten. Of sitting on the porch a warm summer evening. Of homemade lemonade. Of soft laughter. Of the scent of cookies baking. Of holding hands. Of kisses and the promise of what was to come once the kids were in bed and the night was their own.

And then he realized exactly why the images were so strong.

Marnie Jackson reminded him of all he had lost.

"Did you say something?" she asked, jerking him from his thoughts.

Joss swallowed hard. "Ah, no."

But the realization made his insides twitch and as hard as he tried to shake off the feeling, he couldn't. It irritated him. He didn't want anyone reminding him of the life he'd had with Lara. He'd programmed himself to never feel like that with anyone, ever. And really, they were nothing alike. Sure, Lara had the same kind of husky tone, and she always made him own his behavior when he was being a jerk, and she had a wide, tempting mouth. And yeah, they were the same height and had other physical similarities. Lara had always carried a few extra pounds, much to her dismay. But Joss had always thought it made her womanly and sexy. He'd always like curvy women. Tall, skinny women weren't his thing. Except—they were his usual go-to when he went out and hooked up. Which didn't happen that often, anyhow. For a while, a few years after Lara's death, he'd gone through a string of one-night stands. But these days, he was too busy, and simply too damned tired, to make the effort to try and flirt or hook up. And really, he didn't want to be that guy. He wanted to be a man and a father his daughters could respect— not someone who hooked up with faceless women to forget his troubles. Or how much his heart hurt almost 24/7.

The gates to the Triple C loomed ahead and he drove through them, dropping his speed as they headed up the long driveway. No matter how many times he saw it, the ranch always filled him with the sense of family. Even during the bad times, after his mother, Louise, passed away. And then later, when Billie-Jack went off the rails. Even through the terrible time when Hank lay fighting for his life in the hospital and Mitch was trying to keep them all together and out of Social Services…the ranch was an anchor, a place where they could all feel safe.

The house came into view and he heard her sharp intake of breath. It was impressive, he thought, looking at the familiar lines of the large, double-story home with its wraparound veranda and gabled roof, and the large balcony upstairs that gave a spectacular view of the ranch.

"Wow," she said. "What an amazing place."

"Yeah," he agreed and pulled up outside. He could see his brother working with the kids in the largest of the three corrals and suggested they head there once they got out.

A dozen or so chickens scattered as they made their way across the yard, and he weaved a path through the leftover snow and slush on the ground, to where the kids were all on ponies, doing loops around a series of barrels set up in the corral, while his brother stood in the center, giving direction. Joss rested a foot in the bottom tread and noticed that she did the same. Her boots were high-end, suede, definitely not ranch material, and probably cost a small fortune. He wasn't a snob, but he suspected she had money to go along with the poise and education.

"This is on my bucket list." She sighed. "Learning how to ride a horse," she explained. "I don't have a lot of rhythm, though. I mean, I'm a terrible dancer, and as you discovered this morning, will trip over a flat surface."

Joss grinned. "It was slippery."

She gave an agreeable shrug and gestured to the horses. "I guess this came as natural to you as breathing?"

"Pretty much."

"What's that like?" she asked, smiling. "Being good at everything?"

Joss made a scoffing sound. "I'm not. Besides, I could ask you the same thing since you're the one with a PhD."

"But you can ride a horse and play the piano, right? And Clare has bragged about how well you can sing. I can't hold a note. When I was a kid, my cousin and I used to say we were going to be a famous girl band and call ourselves S&M… Yeah, well, that didn't work out because I sound like a howling cat when I sing."

Joss laughed so loud he saw his brother glance in their direction and then thought he must look like he was having a good time hanging out with Marnie. Big mistake. He didn't want any looks. Looks led to speculation.

"Let's go up to the house and I'll introduce you to Tess, my sister-in-law."

He turned and began walking before she had a chance to reply.

By the time they got to the front door, Marnie was almost out of breath. Her shorter steps were no match for Joss's long strides. She followed him inside and had to stop herself from staring as she took in the sight of the incredible ranch house. The polished floors gleamed, and the wide staircase curled around until it disappeared upstairs. There were pictures hung in the stairwell and she fought the urge to race on ahead and have a look. Instead, she walked behind him down the hall, maintaining a discreet distance and trying not to ogle his fine-looking rear end.

There were three women and one man in the huge kitchen. An older woman stood behind the countertop and two younger women were by the table, while the man, who had the same green eyes as Joss and was kind of movie-star handsome, sat on a stool on the other side of the counter.

Joss made the introductions quickly. Mrs. B, who was the housekeeper, Tess, his brother Jake, and Abby, Jake's wife.

My cousin.

The words almost flew from her lips. Marnie

looked at the other woman, searching for similarities, for eye color, hair color. Something. Anything. A way to almost telepathically tell Abby Culhane that they were related. Kin. *Family*.

And then she realized she was now one step closer to reconnecting with her grandmother.

"It's nice to meet you," Tess said and gestured to a chair. "Welcome to the Triple C. And to Cedar River. Clare was telling us you are going to be her new teacher."

"For a while, yes," Marnie replied, conscious that they were clearly all curious about her. Well, she was curious, too.

"Are you taking over the advanced classes from Mrs. Corelli?" Abby asked. "Our son takes her class once a week."

"I believe so. I'll get my full curriculum when I start next week."

"It's a great school," Abby said with a smile. "I'm sure you'll love it there."

"I hope so," she said. She realized that Joss had left the room. And Jake quickly excused himself and disappeared, as well.

"Coffee?" Tess suggested, and within a couple of minutes Marnie's coat was hanging on the back of a chair and she was seated at the table with both women, while Mrs. B hovered behind the counter, preparing food. "So, you're staying with Joss for a few days?"

She saw the query and the curiosity in both women's expressions. "Yes, that's right," she replied and briefly explained about the accident, her double-booked accommodation and the lack of vacancy at the big hotel in town.

"Yes," Abby said and nodded. "I'm head chef at the restaurant at O'Sullivan's. This convention has been booked solid for months. I'm working the dinner shift tonight and the lunch and dinner shift tomorrow. I'll be sure to ask the concierge about any cancellations, but your chances aren't looking good, all things considered."

"The girls told me they've liked having you stay with them," Tess said, her gaze clear and inquisitive. "How are you getting along?"

"With Clare and Sissy?"

"With Joss," Tess specified and smiled.

"Just fine," she replied, heat creeping up her neck. "It was very nice of him to put me up, considering I arrived so early, but he says I'll be in the rental house by Tuesday. I'm looking forward to doing some sightseeing around town. And trying the restaurant at O'Sullivan's," she added and looked toward Abby.

"The food's great," Abby said. Then she laughed and gestured toward Tess. "Just watch this one," she warned, still grinning. "I can see she's got her matchmaking hat on."

Marnie almost spluttered out her coffee. "Ah... what?"

"Don't listen to her," Tess said. "So, you're not married? No boyfriend?"

"Um…no… I recently broke up with someone and I don't think—"

"Exactly," Tess said and chuckled. "That's the trick. Don't think, just go with it."

Marnie was about to make the correction of the century when another woman appeared in the doorway. Younger by a few years, and with a mane of bright red-gold hair and glittering green eyes. A Culhane, for sure.

Ellie Culhane, she discovered moments later. The youngest sibling. A friendly, chatty woman whom she liked instantly. She took a seat opposite Marnie and told Marnie all of her favorite places in town.

"Best restaurant, O'Sullivan's, of course," Ellie said with a wink at Abby. "Rusty's is the best place for dancing and catching up. We usually have a booth seat booked every Friday. I mean, me and my brother Grant and best friend, Winona. But they got married a few months back and are having a baby, so they're kind of in this couple bubble at the moment and are like a boring old married couple now."

"Hey," Tess and Abby said in unison.

Ellie waved a dramatic hand. "You know what I mean. Married people have a way about them. Anyway, if you ever want to go out, Marnie, let me know. I'll give you my cell number before you leave today."

Marnie smiled, amused that she'd found someone who talked more than she did.

An hour later, the lessons were over, the kids were washed up and Mrs. Bailey had set up a buffet-style lunch on the sideboard in the dining room. Clare hovered at her side and Marnie was glad for the company. There were a lot of Culhanes in the room and it was a little overwhelming. She longed for the chance to speak with Abby again, to gather some intel, to find a way to ask questions about Patience Reed.

She placed food on her plate, trying not to feel conspicuous as the only stranger in the room. And Clare, bless her, stuck by her side until she found a place at the table.

And as fate would have it, right beside Joss.

"Everything okay?" he asked when she was seated, him on her right, Clare stuck like glue to her left.

Marnie nodded and felt the sounds around her amplifying as the seconds ticked by. "Yes, of course."

"They're a noisy bunch," he said, quickly interpreting her reaction. "And there's actually a couple of them missing."

"Your twin?"

"Yeah," he replied. "And my youngest brother and his wife."

"Who are in a couple bubble," she said and grinned, looking sideways. "According to your sister."

He groaned a little. "Gotta love Ellie. But she's right."

"I wonder what that feels like," she said quietly and then wished that she hadn't, because his fork stilled midair and he held her gaze with blistering intensity.

"Maybe you'll find out one day."

She shrugged one shoulder. "Maybe. I'm not sure I'm a 'couple bubble' kind of person. I don't think I feel things that deeply."

As soon as she said it, she wanted to snatch the words back. And then realized she did that a lot around Joss. He had a way of getting her to say what was on her mind—and for someone who rarely talked about herself, or her deepest feelings, it was an alien place to be.

"Who was born first, you or your brother?" she asked, shifting the subject.

"Me. Older and wiser, by about seven minutes."

"I'd love to have a sibling."

He discreetly gestured around the table. "Please, have one of mine."

She laughed softly, relaxing a little, and wondered if he knew how brilliantly green his eyes were. "Actually, I'm a little jealous."

His gaze narrowed, and he took a moment, clearly trying to find the right words. "Do you always say exactly what's on your mind?"

"To you?" She sighed. "Seems that way."

"Funny that," he said and speared a piece of asparagus on his plate. "And unexpected."

"Go figure. You're easy to talk to. Which I wouldn't have said two days ago because when you towed my car you were an unbearable grouch."

"In my defense," he said, looking earnest, "even though it's my job, you did drag me out of the house late on a Friday evening. And it was cold and snowing. They're kind of grouchy circumstances, don't you think?"

She smiled. "For sure. It's nice how your whole family has stayed in Cedar River."

"Jake left for a while," he said quietly, so only she could hear. "He was in the army for about ten years. And Grant travels a lot for his work, but he seems settled now he's married and has a baby coming."

"You stayed?"

"It's my home. My kids were born here. My wife is buried here. They're strong reasons to stay. I take it you don't feel that way about California?"

"No. I mean, I like my apartment and my life… but it's never kept me anchored there, if that makes sense."

"It does," he replied. "More than you know."

Chapter Six

Joss was talking to Marnie when he glanced up and saw both of his brothers watching him with keen interest. He knew what they were thinking. He knew what his sister and his sisters-in-law were thinking. He suspected even his daughters were thinking it.

Marnie was the first woman he'd brought to the ranch since Lara had died.

He also knew they were reading way more into it than he wanted.

She was a friend.

No…an acquaintance.

No…a tenant.

Whatever she was, it didn't mean anything.

Except…it felt like it did. Which was damned confusing.

He was pleased when Ellie made some overly dramatic comment about Mitch's business partner, Ramon Alvarez. A rancher from Arizona whom his brother had been working with for the past few years on a shared breeding program, a man that his sister swore she loathed, and who was arriving in Cedar River soon to check out the latest foals born as part of the program.

"All I'm saying is that his horses are not the be-all and end-all," Ellie said pointedly.

"When he arrives, Marnie can speak to him in Spanish," Sissy announced, as though she'd solved some great problem.

Ellie's eyes widened. "You speak Spanish?"

Marnie nodded. "Yes."

Ellie, as inquisitive as a bull terrier, kept asking questions. "Just Spanish?"

He noticed Marnie glance in his direction, then hesitate for a moment, before she replied. "And, well…French and German." She took a breath. "And Italian."

Ellie's already rounded eyes widened even further. "You speak *five* languages? Fluently?"

She looked down at her plate and then glanced back up at the startled expressions around the table. "Ah…yes."

Joss's gut took a sharp dive. Five languages? Was

she some sort of genius? Sure, he knew she was smart and had a PhD…but he'd met smart people before and none of them could speak five languages.

"Marnie is a doctor," Clare said matter-of-factly.

"Medical doctor?" Ellie asked.

"No," she corrected. "I have a PhD in history. It's a title, not a calling."

"You're wicked smart, hey?" he asked once the conversation died down and he was certain no one else could hear.

"Yeah," she said, not looking at him. "Wicked."

"Mensa smart?"

She jerked her gaze sideways, like she was surprised by his question. Or maybe it was that she considered him to be a grunt and wouldn't know what the organization was. "Yes."

"Well, I'm not intimidated by that in the least," he said, deadpan.

"Good," she said and he noticed her mouth curled at the edges. "Don't be."

Once lunch was over and Tess and Abby disappeared into the kitchen with Mrs. B, and his daughters convinced Ellie to show Marnie around the ranch, Joss was stuck enduring the inevitable questions from his brothers.

They headed for the living room and Joss dropped into the single chair by the fireplace while his brothers both sat on the sofa.

"So," Jake said, a humorous glint in his eyes. "A doctor, eh?"

"Don't start," he warned.

"You like her," Mitch said quietly.

"I hardly know her," Joss said and gave them a quick death stare. "Anyway, I think she should stay here until Tuesday. Or maybe with you and Abby," he said, looking at Jake.

"And miss all the fun of watching you do something totally against what you would normally do?" Mitch said, smiling broadly. "I don't think so."

"I have no idea what that means," he said flatly.

"It means, you've been hooking up casually for years, and now Dr. Marnie has landed on your doorstep," Mitch said without batting a lid. "It's about time you dealt with your grief, don't you think? What better way than with a woman who has *more* to offer you other than a night or two between the sheets."

Irritation kernelled in his chest, but he didn't get angry with his brother. He couldn't. Mitch was the one person he respected above all others. "You're way off the mark. I've only known her for two days."

"I'd only known Tess for two hours when I knew she was the one for me."

"That's true," Jake said and grinned. "He called me up and told me."

"Look, I'm delighted you're having this little trip down memory lane, but you're wrong. I'm leasing her a house, that's it. And my *grief*," he said pointedly, "isn't something I want to talk about."

"Lara wouldn't want you to spend the rest of your life alone, you know," Mitch said gently.

"I know," Joss said, suddenly hanging on to his temper by a thread. "But I've already had the great love of my life. I don't expect to ever have that again. I'm not in the market for anything other than a casual thing every now and then. Anything you imagined you've seen today…well, it's exactly that, in your imagination."

"Okay, I hear you," Mitch said, in a fatherly kind of tone Joss had come to recognize over the years. "Just know we're here if you ever need to talk. And if you'd prefer for Marnie to stay here, then of course she's very welcome."

He nodded and then changed the subject. "I did want to talk to you both about something," he said and sighed. "Billie-Jack called me again. And Hank, I haven't responded yet, but I wanted to know how you both feel about it."

"I told him to go to hell," Jake replied bluntly.

Mitch exhaled. "We've talked. I said my piece. And now I can move on with my life. I suggest you do the same."

It sounded too simple, too cut-and-dried. Maybe he was overthinking it? Perhaps Jake had the right idea and telling the old man to take a hike was the right way to go. Still, Joss wasn't one to make rash decisions. He needed time to think about it.

Although, for months now, Joss had avoided thinking about his father. He knew the man was sick and probably didn't have a whole lot of time left, but with two kids to consider, Joss didn't have the energy for any drama.

It was after two o'clock when he finally had the opportunity to round up the girls and Marnie and head home. The girls insisted he turn up the volume when a popular country pop song came on the radio.

"Please, Dad, it's Shay Logan's latest song," Sissy said pleadingly.

Joss didn't know much about the music preteens listened to, but he knew the pop princess was a favorite of both his daughters. He'd rather chew glass than listen to country pop music, but he did as they asked, and they sang along to the lyrics. When the tune was over, he reset the volume.

"You like Shay Logan?" Marnie asked the girls.

"Adore her!" Sissy replied dramatically. "She's awesome."

"Didn't she have a nervous breakdown, or something?" he suggested, remembering he'd read something about her on social media. He wasn't sure she was the type of person he wanted his daughters revering. "Got put in jail for refusing to provide her license or something like—"

"Her husband died," Marnie said, cutting him off.

"And she didn't spend any time in jail. She failed a preliminary breath test, got fined and lost her license. The media made a big deal about the whole incident."

He frowned. "You seem to know a lot about it."

"I do," she replied. "I *should*. She's my cousin."

"Huh?" he said, figuring he sounded dense, because he heard exactly what she said. "Your cousin?"

"Yes, and one of my closest friends."

Code for *so back off*, he figured. And by now Sissy and Clare were asking a whole bunch of excited questions. Sissy, in particular, wanted to know all about it and he endured fifteen minutes of endless chatter about a diva he suspected wasn't quite the innocent victim that Marnie was making her out to be. But she was her family, and people often only saw the good in their kin.

Almost as soon as they pulled up at home, he took off for the house down the street and stayed there until after five thirty. He finished painting the bathroom, managed to patch a couple of small holes in the wall in the laundry and prepped the kitchen for the plumber the following day. When he got back home, he walked around the rear and washed up in the laundry. He really needed to spend some time in the yard, too. The gazebo needed a repaint; the hedges needed trimming. He'd purchased a hot tub the previous summer and rarely had a chance to use it. The truth was, he didn't do much of anything other than work and be a full-time parent. He'd even installed a home gym in one corner of the garage to save time.

Joss headed through the back door and stalled beneath the threshold when he spotted Marnie in the kitchen, clearing away dishes. "Did the girls bail on you again?"

"I gave them the night off," she replied. "Seeing as it's a school day tomorrow. They wanted something light to eat, so I made them mac and cheese. I hope that's okay?"

"Someone cooking other than me? No problem," he added and half smiled. "They've already told you my cooking sucks."

She smiled. "Can I get you anything?"

"Coffee," he said and shook some dried paint out of his hair as he walked across the room. "I'm just gonna shower and get changed first," he said and then lingered in the doorway for a moment. "Ah, Marnie... I was wondering, would you prefer to stay at the ranch until the house is ready?"

Her hands stilled above the sink. "Would you rather I did?"

"No," he replied. "But I wanted to make sure you were still okay with being here."

"I'm okay." She nodded.

Joss didn't wait for anything else and took off down the hallway.

He took a shower, as cold as he could stand, and told himself it was only to clean away the paint and debris from his skin and hair. But he knew it was more than that. He wanted to snap himself out of whatever it was that was going on in his head.

Even though he knew it was crazy. She was in town for only six months, she'd made that abundantly clear. And she was on the rebound from an ex who'd clearly busted her heart to pieces. So, even if she was looking at him in a way that could be considered *interested*, he was positive he was imagining it. Projecting something he wanted to see in her gaze.

Not that he wanted to see anything in her gaze, he told himself. Not at all.

Once he was shaved and dressed, Joss checked on Sissy and Clare, and found Sissy in the office, sitting lotus style on the fold out bed, and his youngest in her bedroom.

"Can you believe that Marnie is Shay Logan's cousin," his daughter breathed on an excited sigh. "That's so awesome. It's almost like we know her, too. And Marnie said she'd try and get an autograph for me."

"Great. So, only an hour of social media tonight," he said to his eldest daughter. "Okay?"

She nodded. "Sure, Dad. I'm going to study for my exam for a while and then probably go to sleep."

"You can watch TV if you like, maybe pick a movie with Clare?"

"Nah, it's okay, I think I'll just stay in my room.

Clare's had her bath, so I'll check on her a bit later and make sure she's in bed by eight."

Joss frowned. "What's going on? You're not usually this agreeable."

She smiled sweetly. "Well, my birthday's in two weeks, remember? I'm trying to be on my best behavior so I can get a new phone."

True, she'd been at him for weeks for an updated cell and he was considering it, but he wasn't completely buying her compliance. "Uh-huh. If that's all it is."

"Of course," she said, still smiling. "Did you know it's Marnie's birthday just a week after mine?"

No, he didn't. And then he read between the lines and suspected his daughter was staying in her room so she could give him a nudge in Marnie's direction. "Ah, honey, you know that once Marnie moves into the house down the street she's just going to be Clare's teacher. I wouldn't be getting any other ideas."

Sissy looked at him. "Ideas?"

He sighed. "You know what I mean."

His daughter shrugged. "She's really cool, Dad. Besides, she likes you. And you like her."

"No," he said gently, shaking his head. "I don't. I mean…yeah, she's a nice person and everything… but that's it. So, no more of this, okay? Good night, see you in the morning."

"Night, Dad, love you."

"Love you more," he said and headed down the hall to Clare's room. His youngest was on her bed, reading a book about horses. "What you up to, kid?"

"Just learning about hoof antomy," she said.

"Anatomy," he corrected and grinned as he sat down beside her.

"Yeah, that." She giggled. "Uncle Mitch said I need to know all of the parts if I want to be a vet when I grow up."

"Uncle Mitch is right," he said, ruffling her hair. "Did you have fun today?"

"I always have fun at the ranch," she said and then sighed. "Daddy, do you think you'll ever get married again?"

What was going on with the people in his life? "Why do you ask, honey?"

She shrugged her small shoulders. "I've just been thinking about it. I mean, it would be okay if you wanted to, that's all."

Joss's chest tightened. "I know you'd like to have a mom. But you know, you had a mom and she loved you more than anything."

His daughter's chin wobbled and she glanced at the framed photograph of Lara on her bedside table. "I don't remember her."

"I know that," he said gently, the ache in his chest intensifying. "But if I did get married again, it would have to be to someone I really liked. And someone you and Sissy really liked, too. Because you and your sister are the most important people in the world to me. And someone *that* special is hard to find."

"But do you think you'd know if you met her? Like, could she be someone you already know?"

"I suppose she could be, yes," he said.

Clare's green eyes widened. "And would you, like, ask her out on a date, or something?"

Dread pressed down on his shoulders, because he knew exactly what his youngest daughter was asking and thinking. "Honey, has this got something to do with Miss Jackson?"

Clare dropped her gaze for a second. "She said I could call her Marnie, except when I'm at school, 'cause then she'll be my teacher and I have to call a teacher Mr. or Mrs. or Miss—that's the rule. I really like her, Daddy."

"Yeah, I know you do. But when you marry someone," he explained gently, "you have to know them really well. And the only way to get to know someone is to spend lots of time with them."

"Like on dates?" she asked curiously.

"Well, that's part of it, yes. Anyway—" he kissed her forehead "—I think we'll save this conversation for another time, okay? Your sister said she'd come and tuck you in a little later."

She nodded. "Daddy, I love you with all my heart."

Joss blinked back the heat in his eyes. Clare was such a loving child, quieter than her sister, almost protective of those she cared about, and he was so proud of the wonderful person she was becoming. "I love you, too, honey."

By the time he was back in the kitchen he could smell coffee and something he was sure was Marnie's perfume, which was like vanilla and apples mixed together. She was sitting at the table, doing something on her phone. She looked up when he entered the room. And he saw it. In her eyes. Behind her glasses. Undeniable.

Attraction.

Joss had never considered himself vain. Sure, he knew he could get a woman's attention if he wanted it, but he didn't spend a whole lot of time thinking he was any better- or worse-looking than the next guy. So, he said the first thing that popped into his head.

"Would you like to go out with me?"

Marnie stared at him, then blinked a couple of times. "What?"

He shrugged loosely, like he was tight in the shoulders and needed to relieve some tension. And there was something in his expression she couldn't quite fathom. Awareness? Attraction? Whatever it was, she wasn't quite prepared for the way it made her feel.

"Would you like to go out with me?"

"Now?" she queried, heat churning through her blood.

"Well, no," he replied quickly. "I meant sometime in the next couple of weeks. Once you're settled into the house."

"You're asking me out on a date?" she said, not quite believing what she had heard.

"Ah…yeah."

She swallowed hard. The introvert in her wanted to do a happy dance, but she didn't. She gathered her composure and nodded. "Well, I think…okay."

"All right, then," he said and moved around the countertop. "We were going to have coffee."

Marnie's feet felt like they were stuck in cement. "And that's it? No more talk about it?"

"No need," he said, grabbing a couple of mugs. "We'll arrange something once you're in the new place. What are your plans for tomorrow?"

"Actually," she said, hoping her cheeks didn't look as hot as they felt, "Ellie is taking me sightseeing for a couple of hours."

"My sister is good company," he said and grinned. "I'm sure you'll get her best tiny-town tour. By the way, I hope I didn't upset you when I made that comment about your cousin."

"No." She got to her feet. "I'm just a little overprotective. People always want to believe the worst of those who're famous. And Shay has been through some tough times. But she's working through it. Sometimes it's hard, though, because the paparazzi are relentless. Whenever my family get together we've had helicopters over our houses with photographers trying to get a photo of her doing something scandalous. The truth is, Shay is one of the least scandalous people you'd ever meet. And one of the kindest."

"It's true when they say fame comes with a price tag."

"For sure," she breathed. "I've witnessed Shay being hounded by the press and she's always polite and so generous with her fans."

"So, she's the famous half of the band S&M?" he queried, smiling broadly.

"The talented half," Marnie corrected and took the coffee mug he passed. "There's leftover mac and cheese in the refrigerator if you're hungry."

"Will you judge me if I tell you I feel like ice cream?"

"Not at all," she replied. "What flavor have you got?"

He opened the freezer. "Fudge Mint or Salted Caramel?"

"Fudge Mint," she replied and soon they were sitting at the table, a spoon each, sipping coffee and sharing a tub of ice cream. "I suppose you can eat anything you like and never put on a pound?"

"Pretty much. You?"

Marnie's brows shot up. "You've got to be kidding. I've never been that lucky."

He shrugged. "No man likes skin and bones anyway."

Marnie tapped the spoon on the edge of the container. "Some do."

"The cheating ex?"

"No," she replied. "Despite what he did, Heath wasn't that superficial. He said looks didn't matter—which is probably a backhanded insult, anyway. But my sad story is that I got rejected by a guy in college because, he said, I was fat."

He winced. "Sounds like a jerk, then."

"He was. But no girl likes to hear that word."

"People who say things like that never realize how much harm they're causing. But never forget that they're jerks for saying it, and it's normal to be upset by those comments," he said.

"That's good advice."

"If my daughters are ever in a situation like that, I hope they talk to someone they trust about how they feel, and they learn to be kind to themselves." His expression was intense.

"I wish I'd heard this when I was a teenager…" she said and sighed. "My dad was more the 'if someone is calling you fat, lose a few pounds, then' kind of parent."

"You're not serious?" Joss asked, looking incredulous.

She nodded and shrugged. "I don't think he meant to be unkind. That was just his way, I guess."

"Do you see him much?"

She shook her head. "Not a lot. He left when I was twelve and got married again a couple of years later. We speak every few weeks, but it's nothing deep or meaningful. What you said yesterday was probably right—I think he feels guilty, but I think he would still have made the same decision to leave. My mom—" she shuddered out a long breath "—she was troubled. She suffered with bipolar disorder and he said she was hard to live with at times. And I guess he believes he had his reasons for leaving, but…"

"But that doesn't make it hurt any less?"

Her throat tightened. "Exactly."

"My father resurfaced a few months ago after nearly twenty years," he said quietly, and then all she could hear was the faint tick of the clock on the wall and the gentle hum of the refrigerator. "He's sick and wants to reconnect."

"Do you?"

"I haven't decided yet," he replied.

"So, what you're saying is that we all have stuff going on in our lives?"

He shrugged. "I'm saying that it's okay to be disappointed in your parents. I'm sure my girls will have their fair share of disappointment in me as they get older."

"I doubt that," she said and met his blistering gaze. "They adore you."

"They want me to get married again."

Marnie held the visual connection. "But?"

"I'm not sure I have it in me," he said. "I loved Lara. I still do. But kids see things easier than adults. They see an empty seat at the dinner table, I see a place where my wife used to sit."

Marnie's insides contracted. She'd never known love like that. And suddenly, she experienced a deep-rooted envy of Lara Culhane. And she wondered, as she shared ice cream and conversation with Joss, if he could read that feeling from her expression. If he did, she would be humiliated, because she didn't want Joss thinking she was swooning or pining or any of that nonsense. Because that was what it was, right? She was being swept away by the fact she was in his house, sharing meaningful conversations. He was nice and friendly and, frankly, gorgeous, and she was a flesh-and-blood woman who hadn't had male attention since forever—no wonder she was hungry for it.

"I think I'll call it a night," she said and got to her feet. "I had a nice day. Thank you for taking me with you guys to the ranch."

He pushed back in his seat. "You're running away?"

"Absolutely," she admitted, coloring hotly. "It's a defense mechanism."

"Against what?"

"Against whatever is going on here," she said and waved a hand between them. "Which is probably all in my imagination, but feels real, nonetheless."

His gaze held hers. "You're not imagining it."

She sucked in a sharp breath. God, she didn't have conversations like this. She wasn't sexy or flirtatious. She didn't know how to be. Her head was already spinning from the fact he'd suggested they go out on a date. He wasn't really interested in her—was he?

"I'm not?"

"No," he replied. "I enjoy your company. I like talking to you."

And that was it. A gal pal...that was what he wanted? He'd already told her he didn't have female friends... Perhaps he was turning over a new leaf and wanted to try her out, so to speak, to see if he could have a woman friend.

"So, before," she muttered, heat crawling up her neck, "when you said we should go out, you meant like, just to hang out? Not a real date?"

"A real date? Are we talking about sex now?"

She gasped, seeing the query in his expression, and thinking no man had the right to look that darn sexy. "Ah, no...of course not. I only meant that the word *date* usually has certain connotations attached to it. Like not splitting the check or holding hands or even kissing good-night...you know...that kind of thing."

Gawd, I wish a giant sinkhole would form under my feet.

He was smiling and she spotted a tiny dimple in

his cheek. Green eyes, ink, dimples…the man had the trifecta of hotness going on.

"Yeah…it would be a real date," he said. "But not yet. Not while you're here and the girls are around. I don't want to confuse things, okay? But who knows what the future might hold."

Kissing? In that moment, Marnie didn't think she'd ever wanted to kiss anyone so much, not ever. She took off like her feet were on fire, afraid to hear any more, or to read any more into his words. So, of course, she had another sleepless night, and when she finally roused the house was empty. There was a note propped up by the coffee machine and a set of keys.

Car and house key. See you this afternoon. J.

Marnie looked at the note and relaxed a little. After breakfast she looked for something to do, but seeing as the house was neat as a pin, she ran out of chores by nine o'clock. Thankfully, Ellie texted soon after and by ten she was in town.

"I'm so glad we're doing this," Joss's sister said when they met up at a bakery for coffee "I needed a break from the ranch. Mitch is a tough boss," she said and laughed. "Not that he's really my boss, either. And he's a great brother. I'm lucky, as all my brothers are wonderful. I asked Abby to snag us a lunch table at O'Sullivan's, and she came through with a one o'clock reservation. I thought I'd show you the school and a few of the sights before we head there."

Marnie had a great morning with Ellie. The other

woman was funny and chatty and they got along so
well that by the time they headed to O'Sullivan's she
felt as though she'd made a solid friendship. Lunch
was divine, and Abby came out to their table to say
hello once the crowd lightened up, around two thirty.
Marnie was immediately tense, but held on to her
nerves. She wanted to talk to her cousin, and then
felt a little guilty for using Ellie, or any of the Culhanes, as a conduit to connect with her cousin. But
it couldn't be helped. That was why she had come
to Cedar River, after all. Not to make friends—but
to find her family.

And she wouldn't let anything derail that plan.

Not even the fact she was in danger of falling for
Joss Culhane.

Chapter Seven

On Thursday, two days after she'd moved into her new house, Marnie finally felt as though she was settling in. Sissy and Clare dropped in to see her every afternoon and she suspected they were a little sad she'd moved out. Joss had also stopped by a couple of times, mostly to ensure the utilities were all in working order.

She was scheduled to start her job at the elementary school on Monday and was eager to get into some kind of life rhythm. She spent some time settling into the house, sorting through her clothes and selecting her outfits for the following week, and then ordered a few items online because she was missing some essential things from her wardrobe—like a down coat and sensible boots.

Her cell pealed after five on Friday afternoon and she picked up immediately when she spotted Shay's number.

"All settled?" her cousin asked.

"Just about," she replied. "New job starts Monday."

"How's the hot single dad?"

"I don't think I actually said he was," she said, not mentioning his suggestion they should go on a date.

"I can read between the lines." Shay chuckled. "How's the local recon going?"

She briefly explained how she'd met Abby a couple of times. "She seems nice."

"And your grandmother?" Shay asked.

"I haven't met her yet," Marnie replied and explained how she was working toward connecting with Patience Reed.

"Just be careful, okay?" Shay warned her. "It's a slippery slope when you start hiding things… Believe me, I know."

"Things will get better for you," Marnie said, hearing the hurt in her cousin's voice. "Maybe you need to take a break?"

"I've been thinking about it." Shay sighed. "Maybe I'll come for a visit like I threatened. You can show me around your new town, introduce me to the locals. It might be all the inspiration I need to start writing some new material."

"I wish I could help you more," Marnie remarked. "I feel bad for taking off right when you needed me the most. But with everything that happened with Heath and then the teaching position here came up and I—"

"Of course, you had to go," Shay assured her. "And I'm fine, I promise. I haven't seen a photographer or reporter for a couple of days, so that's a good sign. Anyway, I have to go, but I'll call you next week."

The call ended and Marnie experienced a pull of longing for her family. And then, inevitably, a deep feeling of loss for her mother. She was still feeling a little blah and walked around the house, closing a couple of windows she'd opened a little earlier to let some fresh air into the house. Which turned out to be a bad idea, because the one in the living room got stuck and she couldn't get it shut, no matter how hard she tried. She gave up after ten minutes and texted Joss.

I have a problem. Living room window won't shut. Do you have time to help out?

Her cell pinged thirty seconds later.

Okay. Be there soon.

For a moment—albeit brief—she considered running a brush through her hair. But didn't get a chance because Joss's truck pulled up out the front of the house.

"That was quick," she said, moving down the porch steps as he strode up the path.

"I was heading home, so I was just around the corner anyway," he said. "What's up?"

She pointed to the front window. "I can't get it to close. I opened it about an hour ago to let in some fresh air, but it's jammed or something."

He hiked up the steps and had the window closed in a couple of seconds. "It should be fine, but I'll get some WD-40 for the tracks."

"Thank you. Ah… I was wondering if you and the girls would like to come over for dinner? Just to say thanks for all your help and for giving me a place to stay. I… I made a huge pot of spaghetti sauce this afternoon."

"The girls are spending the weekend with their grandparents in Rapid City. I just dropped them off."

"Oh, okay. Well, you can still…" Her words trailed and she swallowed hard. "I mean, you probably have plans for tonight anyway, so that's fine, I'll just put it in the freezer and—"

"What time?"

She looked at him. "Huh?"

"What time?" he asked again. "Seven?"

Marnie's skin prickled. "Yes, fine."

"See you then," he said and turned, walking off without another word.

Marnie had over an hour to cancel. Over an hour to think about what she was inviting. Or suggesting. Or simply *thinking*. By the time seven o'clock came, she was changed into fresh jeans and a pale blue shirt and had tied her hair up in a ponytail. She wasn't going to look as though she was *trying*…not a chance. She had the spaghetti sauce simmering, the pasta almost cooked, crusty bread in the oven and music playing in the background. Nothing soft and dreamy or even remotely romantic. It wasn't a date. It was dinner. Between friends.

He arrived a couple of minutes past seven, removing his jacket as he crossed the threshold. In jeans and a dark polo, the tattoo peeking out from the edge of the sleeve. And his hair… Oh, sweet heaven. It should be illegal for a man to have such beautiful hair. He had a bottle of wine in his hand and she managed a smile.

"Ah, dinner's nearly ready," she said and took off down the hallway.

"The place looks good," he said once they were in the kitchen. "Very homey."

Marnie glanced at the few knickknacks she had added. "I bought a few things in town the other day, when I was with your sister. She took me to the antique shop near O'Sullivan's. And we visted the museum and art gallery. It was fun."

"Yes, she said you guys had a nice time."

"Ellie's good company."

He placed the wine on the countertop. "She said the same thing about you."

Marnie grabbed a couple of glasses and he quickly opened and poured the wine.

"I like your hair," she said and then wanted to kick herself for being so obvious. "I mean, it looks...you know how it looks."

He laughed softly. "I had it cut a few months back. My brothers were on my case about how long it was getting. Jake in particular," he added and grinned. "No doubt because he's always preferred that military crew cut."

"Do you have a picture?" she asked, instantly curious.

He nodded and grabbed his cell, flicking through the photographs, and showed her one of himself with his daughters. And yes, he had long hair, tied back at his nape with a thin leather strap. "So you're sexy with short *or* long hair," she said and sipped some wine. "Although, I can't believe you gave in to peer pressure and chopped it off."

He shrugged lightly and grinned. "Sexy, huh?"

Heat blotched her cheeks, but there was no denying it. "You don't need me to tell you that."

He chuckled. "You know, I thought Ellie might have persuaded you to go to Rusty's tonight."

"She tried," Marnie admitted. "But I'm a bit of a homebody—not really a drinking and dancing kind of person. What about you? I thought you said you kicked your heels up on the weekends you didn't have the girls?"

His expression narrowed. "I don't recall actually saying that. And heel kicking isn't really my thing."

Marnie met his gaze straight on. "I meant… I thought… Well, you're a single guy and you can do what you like."

"I can, you're right. I've screwed around," he said bluntly. "A few years after Lara died, I had more one-night stands that I can remember. It's not something I'm particularly proud of, nor do I want my daughters to think random hookups with strangers is a way to make you happy. It's not. But I'm not that guy now, just so you know."

She didn't respond. Instead, she dished out some food and they spent a companionable hour or so talking about neutral things—like music and movies and their work. It was an easy, comfortable conversation and she relaxed more as the time ticked by. Or perhaps it was the food and the wine that made her more at ease. Whatever, she wasn't going to overanalyze every feeling and emotion she had at every turn.

"And you were never tempted to work on the family ranch?" she asked, once the meal was eaten and they were on their second glass of wine.

"Not really. Mitch is the rancher. And I like running my own business."

"You didn't get to go to college?"

He shook his head. "No. As soon as high school

was over, Lara got pregnant and college was off the table."

"Do you have any regrets?" she asked softly.

"About getting married so young?" he queried and then sighed. "Not consciously. I wouldn't trade being married to Lara or having the girls for anything. A college degree couldn't take the place of…" His words trailed off and he met her gaze. "I didn't mean that it doesn't have value. It just wasn't my journey, I guess."

"I feel the same way about marriage and kids," she said and exhaled. "At least, I think I do. Part of me does have some regret."

"You're still young," he remarked. "You have plenty of time to do the marriage and kids thing if you want."

"I suppose. Just have to meet the right guy. So," she said, shifting the subject, "is Joss your real name?"

"Joseph," he supplied. "But only my mom ever called me that."

"What was she like?"

"Her name was Louise," he replied. "She was kind and had a soft voice. She used to sing to me and Hank before we went to sleep. But then Grant and Ellie came along, so the lullabies stopped. I still remember she used to sing this one song, 'You Are My Sunshine.'" He smiled, and she could see the memories in his eyes. "I loved her a lot."

"So, you've lost both of the women you've loved?"

His brows rose a fraction. "Poor me, huh."

"Oh, it's sympathy you want?"

His mouth curled at the edges. "Right now, no—I don't think so."

There was no denying the flirtatious edge to his words. He wasn't hiding it and she wasn't denying it. But they were words with nowhere to go. He said he didn't hook up casually anymore and she wasn't about to start.

"Is this a close-proximity thing?" she asked curiously.

"What?"

"Whatever this is," she continued and waved a hand vaguely. "I'm not really your usual type, am I?"

He shrugged. "I wouldn't think I was yours, either?"

She laughed a little. "You're not," she replied, amazed that she was having such a candid, open conversation with someone she hardly knew. And yet, there were times, like right in that moment, that she felt a connection to him that was quite powerful. "I usually date book nerds or teachers or professors. Although I went out with this IT guy once, but that was a few years ago. I only asked because sometimes people feel a certain way through circumstances. Let's just say we were stuck on a desert island and were the only two people there—regardless of looks, money, education, even baseline attraction. We'd be drawn to one another simply because there was no one else around. Survival of the species and all that. Instinct really, pure and simple."

"Last I looked—" he reached out to grasp her hand "—we weren't on a desert island."

"I know," she said, and looked to where their hands were now linked. "I was using that example for analysis. The thing is, I don't want to be in something that's about convenience or because you're bored or lonely or whatever. And I know I'm probably jumping the gun here, but I just want to get it all out in the open. I find you incredibly attractive," she admitted, hot now from head to toe. "Which doesn't mean I'm going to jump your bones or anything," she said, waving her hand, "even if I've thought about it."

"I'm flattered," he said quietly, his green eyes darkening. "And, Marnie, this isn't about proximity. Maybe it has crept up slowly this past week, but that doesn't make it mean less than one of those instant attraction kind of things. And frankly, I'm not a *fall in fast* kind of guy. With two kids, I can't afford to be."

That was obvious. He was successful, organized and in control of his life. Much like she was, Marnie suspected. At least, for her, on the surface. In that moment, her hand enclosed in his, her heart beating so strongly it was hard to draw breath, she felt as out of control as she ever had.

"This is all kind of new territory for me," she admitted. "In fact, simply talking to a man like you is kind of new."

"A man like me?" he queried. "Do you mean blue collar?"

She shrugged, knowing she should probably remove her hand from his, but was also terrified of losing the connection. Particularly since his thumb was drawing tiny circles on her palm. "That's not what I mean…not really. It might come out sounding that way, but being around you makes me all hot and bothered so I get all…inarticulate."

He chuckled and the sound warmed her down to her toes. "Didn't the professor types get you hot and bothered?"

"No," she admitted. "Turns out I'm new to this hot and bothered thing."

He stood, still smiling, and dragged her to her feet. "Since we're confessing—you'll be the first doctor I've kissed."

Marnie's temperature skyrocketed and she shuddered in a breath. "You're planning on kissing me?"

He moved around the table and drew her closer. "Only if that's okay with you."

He was so tall, and without heels, Marnie had to tilt her head to meet his gaze. She fought the urge to run her fingers through his hair to feel if it was as silky as it looked. "It's okay," she muttered, feeling small and delicate as one arm moved around her and the other held her hand between them.

She'd been kissed before, many times, but she'd never anticipated a kiss more than she did in that moment. Her lips tingled and her belly rolled as a wave of desire thrummed through her blood. Marnie felt a surge of something else rush through her—something she couldn't quite define—something that wasn't only about desire. *Feelings of love.* She thought the words for a fleeting moment and then dismissed them. She wasn't going to start thinking—no, *imagining*—that it was more than some chemical reaction to his obvious good looks and great body. She didn't have time for real feelings. Attraction and sex she could handle. Hell, she wanted it. Why couldn't she have a fling with Joss Culhane? Why couldn't she feel what it was like to have hot and meaningless sex? Other people did it. And she was as flesh-and-blood as the next person.

When his mouth touched hers she was swept up and away. He knew how to kiss. He knew how to hold. He knew that his large hand sitting gently in the indent at the small of her back was both arousing and reassuring. He knew that at first, the gentle pressure of his mouth on hers was all she needed. All she wanted and could handle. Until the seconds ticked by and her body ached for more. He still held her hand, linking their fingers in a way that was so darn erotic it defied belief. And then the kiss deepened, and his sinful tongue rolled with hers and she was utterly and completely lost.

She moaned and as their tongues met again, a deep rush of heat surged down low and she instinctively pressed her hips toward him, in compliance and need, in a vertical dance as old as time.

Ruined for life. That was what she thought as the kiss continued, as his mouth teased hers, as the hand on her back urged her gently toward him, and she knew without a doubt that one kiss would never be enough to satisfy the throbbing need pulsing through her blood and over her skin.

"Wow," she said when he lifted his head and met her quivering gaze.

"I should probably leave," he said, his breath ragged. "Even though it's the last thing I want to do right now."

It would have been easy to ask him to stay—to ask him to spend the night and make love to her. But despite how much her body craved release, Marnie knew she would regret the decision. Dreaming she could handle a casual hookup while she was in his arms and her lips throbbed from his kiss was one thing; living the reality was another thing altogether.

"Yes, it's probably for the best."

He pulled back and gently released her. "I'll see you soon."

"Sure," Marnie said, feeling the absence of his touch the very moment they parted.

"Thanks for dinner," he said, stepping back.

She nodded. "Ah, Joss… I had a nice time."

"Me, too," he said. "I'll call you."

Marnie smiled, then remembered that they'd agreed to go on a date and wondered if he'd mention it. But he didn't. Maybe she should? She was about to gather her courage when he spoke.

"Goodnight, Marnie. Sweet dreams."

He left quickly and Marnie watched him walk down the street through the front window, her lips still tingling from his kiss, her heart suddenly aching, and feeling more alone than she imagined possible.

By late Saturday afternoon, Joss had had almost twenty-four hours to think about his stupidity.

Worst decision ever...

Best kiss ever...

Of course, it couldn't possibly have been the best kiss. He was just thinking that because it had been too long since he'd hooked up with anyone and he was horny. End of story. That was all it was.

Still, he wasn't indiscriminate…and Marnie had the most amazing mouth.

Tired of thinking about it, he was pleased when Hank showed up around four as it took his mind off things. He grabbed a couple of sodas and joined his brother in the living room.

"He called again," his brother said. "Left a message."

Billie-Jack.

"You gonna call him back?" Joss asked.

Hank shrugged. "I don't know. Sometimes I think it would be easier just to meet up and get it over with, like Grant did. But I'm not sure I want to see him."

"Not surprising," Joss remarked. "Considering what he did. Or didn't do."

Eighteen years later, he still didn't understand why their father had left Hank in a truck as it caught on fire. Thank God Jake had the foresight and good sense to follow the truck on his motorcycle, knowing that Billie-Jack was drunk behind the wheel. Jake had arrived just in time to pull Hank from the wrecked truck, but his twin had still received burns to 30 percent of his body and spent years in and out of hospital.

"Grant talked to him about it," Hank said and shrugged again. "He said he couldn't remember much about the accident. Shock, maybe. I don't know."

"It's no excuse," Joss said irritably. "I've got two kids and if they were trapped in a burning vehicle, I'd do whatever I had to do to get them out—even if it meant giving my life. That's what you do for your kids. He was just too drunk to know any better."

Hank looked at him. "What's eating you?"

"Nothing."

His brother knew him better than anyone. "Spill."

"I did a dumb thing last night," he admitted.

Hank's brow hiked up. "What was that?"

He swallowed. "I made out with Marnie."

His brother grinned. "That's it?"

"For a woman like her, that's enough," he replied, thinking that he'd behaved like a complete ass and if she'd asked him to stay the night, he would have. And then it would have been an even bigger mess.

"Are you gonna see her again?" Hank asked intuitively.

"I'm thinking about it." He laughed humorlessly. "That's the kicker, isn't it? I don't date—we both know this. Dating makes everything complicated."

"But?"

"But the girls really like her," he replied.

"Do you like her?"

He nodded. "Yeah."

"Then what's the problem?"

He tried to think of as many as he could. "She's only in town for six months."

"Plans can change," Hank said.

"Well, I guess. She'll be Clare's teacher."

"She's not *your* teacher, so I don't think that matters."

Sometimes he hated his brother's relentless logic. "She's just come out of a bad relationship."

"How long ago?"

He shrugged. "I'm not sure. A few months."

"So, not exactly rebound stuff?"

"Well, no," he replied. "But she's really not my—"

"You're not going to say she isn't your type, are

you?" Hank asked and rolled his eyes. "Really? Lara was, what—smart, funny and kind? This woman seems to have similar qualities, correct?"

"Yes," he admitted. "Your point?"

Hank chuckled. "My point is that you've met someone you like, and you're backpedaling at a hundred miles an hour. Why?"

"I don't know," he replied. "It's too fast. I've only known her a week."

"Then get to know her better. Ask her out, date each other for a while."

Joss rolled his eyes. "I can't believe I'm taking dating advice from someone who's never had a serious relationship."

"That's because I'm a nice guy and women always stick me in the friend zone," Hank said with a grimace. "Damned irritating. You, on the other hand, are like catnip for women."

"I haven't dated anyone seriously since Lara died," he acknowledged, and his brother nodded. "That's a huge step."

"You mean falling in love again?"

He scowled. "I hate it when you're right, you know that?"

Hank nodded and grinned. "I always was the smart one."

"And that's another thing," he said, looking for excuses. "She's like a genius or something. She speaks five languages and has a PhD. I'm a grunt who fixes cars for a living. It's not exactly a match obvious to the world, is it?"

"You're an idiot," Hank said and shook his head. "Does she like you?"

Heat crawled up his neck. "I think so."

"Then ask her out."

"I sort of did already." He shrugged. "I mean, we didn't make firm plans, but she said she'd go."

"Then why are we having this conversation?" Hank inquired.

"I don't know," he said on an exasperated breath. "After we kissed, I guess I freaked out."

"Since when have you been so afraid of girls?" Hank asked, laughing softly.

"Never," he replied. "*That's* what's freaking me out. I like her, okay," he admitted. "I didn't at first, but I'm realizing more and more that I like her a lot. You're right, she's smart and funny and great to talk to, and she's got the most amazing mouth and her eyes are this incredible blue color and she has this calm sort of way about her that is so relaxing. But I don't want to start something that might not go anywhere. I don't want the girls getting attached to her if it doesn't work out. And yeah," he said unsteadily, "I don't want to get attached to her if it doesn't work out, either. And like I said, she's just come out of a bad relationship and I don't—"

"I think you're *overthinking* this. Just call her up and ask her out. Because if you don't," Hank said, raising his eyebrows, "you know some other cow-boy in this town will."

And that, Joss thought, wasn't something he wanted to happen.

At seven o'clock Saturday night, Marnie got a text message from Joss.

Feel like breakfast tomorrow morning?

She stared at the message. Was this their date? Breakfast? She replied after a few moments.

Sure.

Pick you up at nine-thirty. J.

So, Marnie had a breakfast date. Or maybe it was more like brunch? Anyhow, she'd agreed to Joss's invitation and then spent a ridiculous amount of time on her appearance the following morning. Black pants that fit snugly and that she'd always thought made her butt look good, and a red silky shirt she wore tucked in, with a belt, to highlight her waist. She wore her highest heels—a pair of black ankle boots she'd paid a fortune for and rarely worn. And dabbed on a little makeup—not too much because she didn't want to look like she was trying too hard. She straightened her hair and wore her favorite earrings, and lastly added a long black wool coat that buttoned up the front, that she'd purchased at a clothing store in town the day she'd spent with Ellie. She added knitted gloves and matching scarf and paced up and down the hallway until he arrived.

When he greeted her at the door at nine thirty Sunday morning, her insides fluttered at the appreciative way his gaze slid over her. He looked good, too—in dark jeans, a long-sleeved, white twill shirt that did nothing to disguise his broad shoulders, a sheepskin lined coat and cowboy boots.

"You look great," he said and his gaze lingered at her feet. "But you might need to rethink the shoes since more snow has been predicted for this afternoon."

"I've got that covered," she said and pointed to a bag by the door. She picked up the bag and showed him the contents. "I ordered a sturdy pair of snow shoes from a store in Rapid City, just in case. I have a thing for shoes," she admitted and grinned.

"How many pairs do you have?" he asked.

"Here?" she said and laughed. "As many as I could fit in my luggage. About fourteen pairs," she admitted and returned his grin. "But back home—too many."

He laughed warmly. "So, are you ready?"

She nodded and grabbed her totc, quickly locking up. "Where are we going?"

"A real life honky-tonk," he replied when they were in his vehicle.

She eyed him curiously. "What's that?"

"A Western-style restaurant. There's one not too far out of town and they serve breakfast until midday. If you like it, I'll take you back there for dinner sometime."

True to his word, the restaurant was indeed a Western-themed establishment, right down to the gingham cloths on the tables, the wagon wheel light fittings and the peanut shells on the floor.

She ordered an absurdly large triple cheese omelet with buttered sourdough toast, and he had some kind of mixed grill meal that was almost overflowing on the plate.

"I don't think portion control is important here," she remarked once the waitress had delivered their food.

He laughed softly and then asked more seriously, "How are you feeling about tomorrow? Nervous?"

"A little," she replied. "I haven't started a new job for a few years."

"This is something of a step-down for you, correct?"

She nodded. "Yes…but I'm looking forward to some real teaching. Don't get me wrong, I love teaching at college, but younger kids absorb knowledge like a sponge, and they accept learning more easily and without too much cynicism. At least, that's what I'm hoping for."

"I'm sure you'll be great."

She relaxed and tried not to think about *it*.

The kiss...

And how she wanted more.

She wondered if he'd spent much time thinking about it. And she also wondered if he'd kiss her again.

When they finished their meals and lingered over coffee, Joss suggested they visit his brother Jake.

"He and Abby have a house on the river. All the rich folk live on the river," he added and grinned. "A couple of the O'Sullivans have houses there. It's worth a trip to see how the other half live."

"Your brother's rich?"

"He started some kind of high-tech security firm when he left the military."

They were still talking about it when they headed off a little while later. "You all went off in different directions," she said of his siblings, "and yet you also all came back here. That's really something."

He nodded and then began talking about different places of significance. "You have to see Mount Rushmore and Crazy Horse Memorial, of course."

"And that big rock," she added excitedly. "The one that was in that Spielberg movie—the space movie. It's called Devil's Tower, right? Except I think it's in Wyoming, so I'll have to wait until I have time to go."

He laughed loudly. "It was science fiction and called *Close Encounters of The Third Kind*. And it's only about an hour and a half drive, so if you have a hankering to see it, we could go one day."

She took another sip of her coffee. "You like science fiction, I suppose?"

He nodded. "Naturally. What about you?"

"I love a good rom-com," she replied and chuckled. "But I love a good thriller, too."

"I like old movies, too," he said as they left the parking lot. "You know, the black and white ones that get shown on TV late at night."

"Bogie and Bacall?"

His gaze widened. "You, too?"

"Of course," she replied. "Love them. In fact, I have a bunch of them on DVD."

He smiled, and she experienced a deep sense of kinship in that moment. She wouldn't have imagined it possible to forge such an intense connection with someone in such a short space of time. As they chatted some more, about old movies and aging movie stars, she realized they had a lot of common interests, despite their obvious differences.

They drove through town and across the bridge and Joss told her how the town used to be two separate towns until they merged about five years earlier.

"It was better for business," he said as they turned off and followed the river road. "And for real estate and for local council and the schools. It took some doing to convince some of the older residents that it was the best thing for the town, but eventually the majority won out."

She nodded. "People power. I like that."

They turned off down a long driveway with a high-security gate. Joss punched in the code and they were quickly driving down another length of driveway. A huge house loomed ahead—two stories, constructed from timber and glass. And it had an incredible view of the river, just as Joss had said.

"My goodness," she said as they pulled up outside the house. "Amazing."

"Yeah, it's a nice spot."

"That would be a great place to ski," she said, pointing to the river.

"You ski?"

"Love it," she replied. "I don't get to do it often enough. You?"

"I'm not much of a water baby. Snow skiing, now, that's different. And snowboarding."

"We don't get a lot of snow in California," she said and made a sad face. "I can teach you how to water-ski if you like, once the weather warms up."

"I didn't realize you were planning on staying for summer?"

"Spring, then," she offered. "And perhaps you can teach me to snowboard."

"It's a deal."

Her insides flipped over. "Okay, then."

A moment later Jake appeared on the steps and they got out of the vehicle. They were ushered inside, and once Abby appeared from the kitchen, Marnie was given a quick tour of the house. "It's such a beautiful place," she said as she admired an array of photos on the fireplace mantel. One picture grabbed her attention. It was Abby, standing beside a tall, attractive woman in her seventies. Marnie knew instantly who she was looking at—she had several pictures in the file from the private investigator.

Patience Reed…her grandmother.

"That's my Gran," Abby said, coming up behind her. "She's my rock."

Marnie's chest tightened and she swallowed the heat burning her throat. And she said exactly what was on her mind.

"I'd like to meet her."

Abby's brows rose. "You would?"

Marnie's instinct was to backpedal. Now wasn't the time to divulge anything. "Well… I mean, I'm open to meeting as many people as I can, since I'm new in town."

Abby smiled and nodded. "Well, if you like to play bridge, then Gran is who you need. She nails the other competitors at the local tournaments. She's also in the local theater group and a book club."

Marnie's insides contracted. "She sounds like quite a woman."

Abby nodded. "She is. I couldn't imagine living my life without her."

Like I've had to...

The words hovered on the edge of her tongue. But it wasn't the time for any kind of announcement about who she was and why she was really in Cedar River. Soon, however, she would have to come clean. The more involved she became with Joss, the more important it was for the truth to come out.

Which might, she suspected, turn out to be the biggest risk of her life.

Chapter Eight

"Everything okay?"

Joss sat down next to Marnie on the sofa while Jake and Abby disappeared to make coffee. She looked a little off, unhappy almost, and he was instantly concerned.

"I'm fine," she said and smiled.

Their thighs touched, but she didn't pull away, didn't move, and it occurred to him that only two people completely comfortable with one another would sit like that. A couple. He hadn't been part of a couple for so long he'd forgotten how much he liked it. Even though logic told him to back off, to go slow, that it didn't happen in a little over a week...

inside, in the deepest part of himself, he was thinking and feeling something else altogether.

"So, the Templetons are putting their place on the market," Jake said when they returned, carrying a tray each. "Three properties down from here, right where the river takes on that second bend. Nice house, four bedrooms, single story but set up high on the land, about one and a half acres. He put a new jetty and boathouse in last year. Interested?"

Joss nodded vaguely. He'd been considering moving for a while and had always liked this part of town. He knew the girls would love living by the water. But...moving from the home he'd shared with Lara didn't sit quite right. Or maybe it was just the idea of setting up in a new place, alone, without someone at his side.

"I'll talk to Leola," he said and shrugged. Leola Jurgens was the Realtor in town and managed all of his rental properties. "Maybe I could renovate and sell."

"Or renovate and live in it," Jake suggested.

"You want to move from Mustang Street?" Marnie asked.

"I've been thinking about it," he replied and was pleased Abby changed the subject to Marnie's new job.

"T.J. is looking forward to taking the advanced classes," Jake said.

"Where is he today?" Joss asked.

"With Gran," Abby supplied. "She has him some Sunday mornings for a few hours, when he's not at the ranch having a riding lesson. They both love spending time together. The girls are with Lara's parents this weekend?"

He nodded. "I have to collect them at four o'clock."

"Are they still giving you a hard time?" Jake asked.

"No more than usual."

They hung around for another hour, talking about the town, the hotel and the kids. When they left, Abby made Marnie promise to stop by the restaurant to catch up.

"They're so nice," she said once they were back in the truck and on their way home.

"I think so. You seemed to have really hit it off with Abby."

"Ah…yeah. Better than I…" Her words trailed off and she cleared her throat. "I mean, she's great. I thought you had a good relationship with your in-laws."

It wasn't posed as a question, but he heard the query in her tone. "It's complicated. They tried to get custody of the girls after Lara died."

She gasped. "Why would they do that?"

"Because they'd lost their daughter and they weren't convinced I was a good enough parent to go it alone."

"But they must know you are now?"

"They keep a watchful eye," he replied. "I was twenty-three and they doubted I'd step up. Maybe they thought I was too much like my own father."

"Your father was a drunk and bailed, didn't he? I'd say you were absolutely *nothing* like him."

"I hope so. I know I would never abandon my kids."

"The girls adore you and rightly so. If I ever have children, I hope I have them with someone who is as good a father as you are."

Joss's chest tightened a little. What was she saying? He didn't want to read anything into it…didn't want to overthink anything. "That might be the nicest thing anyone has ever said to me. So, do you want kids?"

It was the million-dollar question, wasn't it?

"One day," she said quietly. "I mean, yes, I'd like to have a baby. Maybe two. The truth is, I've been thinking about it more, especially since my mom died. Wondering if I've spent too much time concentrating on my career and not enough time getting a life."

"You shouldn't think that," he said. "There's room in everyone's life for both. Just because you're a woman doesn't mean you can't have a career *and* a family. I don't want my girls to ever think they can't have both."

She reached out and touched his arm for a moment

and Joss felt the connection through to his bones. "Well, maybe one day I'll be lucky. What you said the other night is true, I guess—who knows what the future holds."

Strangely, he'd been thinking about the future a lot in the last few days. And about his past. About Lara and Billie-Jack. About moving forward...about letting someone in.

"So, you're really thinking about moving to this side of town?"

He got his thoughts back on track. "Maybe."

"For the rich, you said?" she asked, eyes wide. "That's you?"

"Let's just say I've invested wisely over the years," he supplied. "I would probably have to sell the house we're in now, though, and one of the rentals."

"How many rentals do you own?"

"Three, plus a little commercial real estate."

"That's quite a portfolio for someone so young. You're...what?...thirty-three?"

"Thirty-two. You?"

"I'm coming up to the big three-O in a couple of weeks."

"Any plans?"

"Not so far." She shrugged.

Joss sighed. "Marnie...about the other night... I didn't *want* to leave, you know. But since we've only just met—"

She cut him off. "It was just a kiss, Joss…no big deal."

"Really?" he shot back, his ego taking a tiny hit. "No big deal?"

"I mean, it was nice, and I like kissing as much as the next person and you're good at it, so it wasn't exactly a hardship kissing you back. But you're right, we don't know each other very well and I'm trying to settle into this new life in a new place. And you have two kids to consider and don't want to jump into anything too quickly." She looked at him sharply. "Isn't that what you've been thinking?"

"Well…yeah."

"Great," she said and sighed, as if in relief. "We're on the same page."

He doubted that. All day he'd been distracted by her perfume and the way she walked and the sweet temptation of her mouth that he was itching to kiss again. And more.

"It's Sissy's birthday next Saturday and we're having a party for her at the ranch—would you like to come?"

"Very much."

"And don't make any plans for your birthday, okay?" he said, dropping his voice an octave. "I'd like to spend the day with you."

On Monday, Marnie started her new job and had a fabulous day. She spent the morning getting to know her students, doing some reading and discussing lessons related to an upcoming class trip. At lunch break, Clare hung back in the classroom once all the other students were gone, and then again when the day was over, and Marnie was collecting her things.

"Dakota Harris thinks she knows everything," Clare announced as she perched on the edge of a desk.

"That's probably a little unkind," Marnie said.

Clare shrugged her narrow shoulders. "Sometimes she's mean to me."

"I understand," Marnie said quietly. "But it's not okay to be mean back, is it?"

Clare let out a long breath. "I suppose. Daddy says the same thing," she replied, her small mouth twisting to one side. "Ah—Marn... I mean, Miss Jackson...can I ask you something?"

"Sure."

"Do you like my dad?"

She stilled in her seat. "Of course, I like all of you."

"No," Clare said and flapped her hands. "Do you *like* him? Like, *love* him, like him?"

She wanted to deny it. She wanted to shout out that the kid was way off the mark and after a week a person didn't have those kinds of feelings. She'd known Heath for almost a year before she started having real feelings, and they'd been dating for months—*sleeping* together for months—before she dared say the L word. Not a week. Sure, it had been an intense week—but still only a matter of days. And yeah, she'd had a lovely day with him on Sunday. And yeah, he'd kissed her again when they parted and it was mind-blowing and delicious and left her longing for more. But great kisses aside, Marnie wasn't the kind of person who rushed into things. Even coming to Cedar River had been a planned and calculated move that she'd deliberated over for months.

"You know, grown-up feelings are complicated and it's sensible to take things slow."

Clare didn't look convinced. "Even when you've met someone you really like, shouldn't you tell them? I mean, what if something happens?"

"What kind of something?" Marnie asked, digging deeper.

"I don't know…like what if someone dies or something. People die all of the time," Clare said softly. "Like my mom."

Marnie knew she couldn't brush over Clare's concerns and fears. She was her teacher and more than that, her friend, and she cared about the youngster.

"You're right," she said gently, moving around to sit on the edge of the desk so they were facing one another. "People do die—people we love—people we think will be with us forever. Like how you lost your mom, and how I lost my mom. And it's sad and it hurts and we get mad about it and mad with them and we cry and that's okay. We're allowed to be mad and be hurt and cry."

"Even when it makes us feel bad?"

"Even then," she assured her.

"But how can I be mad at someone I don't remember?" Clare asked, so quietly and with so much pain it made Marnie's heart ache for her.

"Because she *was* your mom and you're allowed to miss her and wish she hadn't died. You're allowed to be mad at her, too, for leaving you. And it doesn't matter that you can't remember her very well. You're a part of her memories and you always will be. You can still love her, even though she's not here."

Clare's eyes were glistening brightly, like she'd just admitted something that was secret and sacred to her, and then more words tumbled out. "I wish I had a mom now. My best friend, India, she has a mom *and* a stepmom, and they get to do all kinds of great things together—like go to the mall and hang out and look at dresses and stuff. I know Daddy will take me shopping if I ask him, 'cause he takes Sissy when she says she needs stuff."

Marnie turned in her chair and took hold of Clare's hand. "And you're so lucky you have a such a wonderful dad."

"I know," Clare said. "But I just wish—"

"It's okay to wish for things," Marnie said, gently cutting her off. "As long as you remember to be grateful for all the good things you have."

Marnie heard a noise and looked toward the door, spotting Joss filling the doorway, in work clothes, looking scruffy, soiled and undeniably masculine.

"Hey, Dad!" Clare announced and slipped off the desk, blinking the tears away.

"Hey, kiddo, have you had a good day?"

"The best," she replied and grinned. "Miss Jackson rocks as a teacher."

He smiled and Marnie's belly did a silly and familiar dive. "Go and wait in the truck, will you?"

"Okay, Dad. Bye, Miss Jackson," she said, suddenly cheerful as she raced from the room.

He stepped into the room and she straightened. "How much of that did you hear?"

"Enough to know she's hurting."

"She's just trying to work out her feelings."

"She's not the only one," he said rawly and then shook his head. "Erase that comment, will you? So, how did your first day go?"

"Great," she replied. "The faculty are really nice, and the kids were charming and mostly well-behaved."

"So far, so good, then?"

She nodded. "I think so. And Clare was such a wonderful help."

"Thank you for talking to her," he said.

"My pleasure. She's an amazing girl. She's kind and generous with herself."

"She's her mom."

Marnie smiled. "She's you."

Color spotted his jaw and he shifted on his feet. "Well, I gotta go. We'll talk soon, okay?"

She nodded and watched him leave, feeling a little bereft then for the remainder of the afternoon. By the time she got home it was after five, since she stopped off at the supermarket to pick up some supplies. She cooked a quick chicken stir-fry for dinner and by seven was showered, changed and sitting on the sofa. She was flicking channels on the television when her cell pinged with a text message.

Can I completely overstep the bounds of our relationship and ask a favor? J

She stared at the message and then quickly replied, Sure. Fire away.

A few minutes later, another text came through.

Clare wants a new outfit for the party on Saturday. I asked her if she'd like to go with Tess or Ellie and she said she'd prefer to go with you. I know it's asking a lot, but would you mind taking her shopping one afternoon this week? There are a couple of clothing stores in town that sell kids stuff.

Marnie wasn't sure it was such a great idea, but the thought of disappointing the sweet, motherless child was unthinkable. She replied with a thumbs-up emoji and set the date for Wednesday afternoon after school and then spent the following couple of hours regretting her decision because she knew Clare was getting attached to her and it was all happening so fast. Until she received another text from Joss a little after ten and all her resistance disappeared.

Thanks again. Nite x

As it turned out, the next couple of days flew by and the shopping expedition in Cedar River on Wednesday was a lot of fun. There were two stores in town that sold a selection of kids clothing and after forty minutes of agonizing over a choice between a pink outfit and a bright orange ensemble, Clare thumbed her nose up at the traditional and went with the orange—a bright, layered tulle skirt and a fashionable, stretchy cotton top in autumn hues that matched perfectly. Next, a sparkly denim jacket and ankle boots with a tiny heel. Clare looked adorably grown-up as she paid for the purchases with a credit card obviously supplied by her father. Marnie splurged and purchased a couple of things, including a lovely deep red sweater with buttons and a new pair of jeans.

Afterward, they headed for the bakery for a milkshake and a mini-muffin, and ran into Abby and T.J. doing exactly the same thing. The young boy had been in Marnie's advanced class the previous afternoon and she'd found him to be a clever youngster. He was polite, too, and greeted them with a smile as Abby asked if they wanted to join them. The kids quickly raced toward the large cabinet that held all the ice cream cakes.

"You two look like you've been having a fun afternoon shopping?" Abby remarked, eyeing the bags at their feet under the table.

"We did." Marnie smiled. "Clare needed something for Sissy's party on Saturday."

Abby nodded and kept a watchful eye on the children. "You're coming, of course?"

"Joss invited me," she replied, coloring hotly.

"Lara and I were on the same soccer team when we were kids," Abby said unexpectedly. "It was such a sad thing, what happened to her. I know the family rallied around Joss and the kids. They have that survival instinct ingrained in them, I suppose, particularly after the accident and their father leaving town."

"The accident?"

"The one when Hank nearly died. They don't talk about it much," Abby said and sipped her drink. "Too painful, I suppose. And of course, now that Billie-Jack has come back, it's bringing all those feelings to the surface." She smiled, and sighed. "I'm grateful that my own family is way less complicated."

Marnie almost choked on her drink. *I'm your family.* But she didn't say it. Didn't do anything other than nod agreeably and wish she had the courage to admit the truth there and then. But it wasn't the time. She needed to meet Patience Reed first.

"It's lovely that you're so close to your grandmother." As she spoke she felt hollow inside, but wouldn't allow Abby to see it.

"I'm lucky," Abby replied. "I'm not sure how much you know, but I raised T.J. alone for the first five years. It's a complicated story." She nodded. "Jake and I dated in high school and then broke up. A couple of years later I married his best friend, Tom. But Tom died a few years later and Jake and I...reconnected. T.J was the result and when he returned to town a couple of years ago, we got back together. But without Gran, I'm not sure how things would have turned out." She sighed. "What about your family?" she asked, still watching the kids as they began counting the cookies in the jars on top of the counter.

"My mom died eight months ago. We were very close," she said blankly, cursing the familiar sting behind her eyes. "My parents divorced when I was young, and my dad remarried. I have a couple of cousins that I'm close to."

"I don't have any cousins. My dad had a brother who was a priest and my mother is an only child."

No, she's not...she had a sister.

She wanted to say it so badly the words burned on the edge of her tongue. But something held her

back. Something she knew she would have to face…
and soon.

In retreat mode, she called to Clare and made up
some excuse about having to get home. The SUV
that Joss had loaned her was zippy and good to drive
and she would almost miss it when her own vehicle
was repaired—which was just a couple of days away
according to Joss.

"There's Daddy's work," Clare said and pointed
to a road off Main Street.

Curious, she turned in to the street and pulled up
outside the auto repair shop. His tow truck was there,
and his Ranger was parked out front. Marnie spotted
her own car inside and up on a lift, and Clare was
quick to get out of the vehicle and race inside. Joss
was standing beside a large black Silverado, wearing overalls and work boots, his hair falling over his
forehead, and a streak of grease ran down his cheek.

He looked wholly and utterly masculine and any
other man she'd ever known suddenly paled into in-
significance. Blue collar, he'd called himself. And
she was discovering she liked blue collar, very much.

"Ladies, how was the shopping?"

"Awesome," Clare said excitedly. "I have the best
outfit for the party. And Marnie bought this really
nice sweater with buttons all the way down to here,"
she said and gestured up and down the center of her
chest.

Joss met Marnie's gaze immediately and she knew

what he was thinking. About buttons and sweaters and things that made her turn hot all over.

"Do you want me to take Clare home? I know you're picking Sissy up from dance class this afternoon, so Clare can stay with me until you get her, if you like."

"Sure," he said and wiped his hands on a towel. "We're having enchiladas for dinner if you'd like to join us?"

Marnie smiled. "Thanks, but I have a whole stack of quizzes that I have to grade."

He didn't flinch. "No problem. And thank you for taking her today."

She met his gaze, unsure why she was refusing the invitation, since marking a couple dozen papers was probably half an hour's worth of work. Maybe it was the unease sitting in her stomach after spending time with Abby? Maybe it was simply that she had a need to be alone for a while. Whatever the reason, he accepted it without question, and she knew that was because he wasn't deeply invested in her.

Me, on the other hand...

The more she saw him, the more she wanted him—it was that simple.

She found herself thinking about Joss when she should have been doing a hundred other things. She found herself dreaming, fantasizing, wondering where things might go if she plucked up the courage and told him what she was feeling. Only, she skirted around him and it, afraid of looking foolish, of making things appear more than they were.

And then ultimately, of being rejected.

Like she'd been rejected by Heath, when he'd cheated on her. Because even though she was the one who had ultimately broken things off, he'd bailed from their relationship the moment he slept with someone else.

And then, if she scratched a little deeper, if she pushed past Heath, she realized her feelings had a familiar sting to them—like when she'd been rejected by her father. Even though she knew how difficult things had been between her parents, she still hadn't quite forgiven her father for leaving them.

For leaving me...

Once the thought was out, she felt better, like she'd turned a corner, somehow. For eighteen years she'd told herself she had forgiven her father for walking out—when in fact, she knew she hadn't. Because her mother had taken his leaving so badly, Marnie had hung on to her own resolve, even from such a young age, and become the strong one. The one her mom relied upon. The one her father could leave in charge of things. But all she had done was bury her fears and resentment deep down. Heath's betrayal had opened the wound and moving to Cedar River had suddenly galvanized what she knew—that she was afraid of being rejected. And in particular, now that she was into something with Joss, she was afraid of being rejected by a man she was seriously falling for. And the idea of knowing how broken she'd be if it didn't work out scared her to death.

Joss had to admit it, Ellie and Tess certainly knew how to throw a birthday party. Really, he'd had very little to do with it, other than agree to the invitation list. His sister and sister-in-law had taken the reins and done everything else. All he had to do was show up with a gift and he knew they wouldn't have it any other way.

Just as well, really. Because he had stuff on his mind.

Billie-Jack, for one, who was back in Cedar River for a few days and wanted to talk to him. This time, the message had come through via the social media account for the workshop. It had felt even more intrusive, as though his father had taken a step in his direction without his permission. The truth was, he didn't want drama. He didn't want to be reminded of those days.

He bundled the girls in the SUV around eleven, collecting Marnie on the way. They'd been texting most evenings, once the girls were in bed and he wasn't wandering around the house like a piece of loose change. He'd never had trouble keeping busy before. He'd never had much trouble sleeping, either. But he'd had a restless week, feeling on edge, distracted, like he was caught up in something he couldn't quite define.

She felt it, too, he was sure of it. He was also certain she had stepped back, pulled away from both him and the girls over the course of the past few days. It was nothing overt, just a sense he had. And probably for the best. But when he saw her, walking down the pathway in dark jeans and a bright pink shirt that accentuated her amazing curves, he was almost lost for breath. Her hair was up and the ponytail swished as she walked. And he had never thought glasses were particularly sexy—but on her, they added an extra layer of appeal that knocked him senseless.

"Is everything all right?" she asked once she was in the seat beside him, her perfume knocking him senseless.

"Sure," he lied, and hoped the three females in the car couldn't hear the way the word came out on a strangled breath.

"Hey, birthday girl," she said and turned toward the back, the action pulling on her shirt and exposing way more skin than he figured she intended. He looked away, straightening his gaze to the road ahead, ignoring the twitch racing through his limbs. It was hardly appropriate to be having X-rated thoughts when his daughters were in the back seat. Resentment set in and he stayed quiet on the trip to the ranch, only relaxing when they were finally driving through the gates of the Triple C.

The party was set up in the barn, as per Sissy's request, with long tables covered in checked cloths and a small dance floor set up in one corner. She'd invited most of her class, and as guests began arriving, he figured they'd all said they were coming. Several sets of parents were also invited, people he knew from school and the PTA, friends he'd made over the years. And every Culhane had turned up for the celebration. If any of his family thought it strange that he'd turned up with Marnie, no one said anything. They were, he suspected, pleased to think he was dating someone. Not that they were actually dating—it just seemed that way.

"This is amazing," Marnie breathed as they headed for the gift table and she placed a small parcel alongside the array of wrapped presents already there. He'd relented and bought Sissy the new cell phone she'd asked for, and she'd already set it up and couldn't wait to start taking selfies with her friends.

"Yeah, Ellie and Tess are the party queens. You should see what they come up with when someone gets married."

She jerked her glance in his direction and he immediately felt like an idiot. Weddings? Really. What the hell was wrong with him? "Ah—you know what I mean," he muttered and walked off a little, leaving

HELEN LACEY

183

her flanked by his daughters, who were also looking at him like he'd gone a little crazy.

Sissy wandered off to be with some of her friends and he noticed how Marnie had gravitated toward Abby and the two women were quickly deep in conversation.

Someone slapped him on the shoulder and he turned to see Hank at his side.

"Good to see you've come to your senses," his brother said.

"What senses?"

Hank gestured toward Marnie. "Your date."

"I'm not sure this is a date," he said flatly. "Actually, I'm not sure what any of it is."

He was still thinking about it a couple of hours later, when the party was in full swing, when food and soda were being consumed in copious amounts, when gifts were being opened, when the cake arrived and the joy on his daughter's face was palpable.

He was sitting at the table with Hank and with both his daughters eating cake, when Marnie joined them, squeezing in between both girls.

"Thank you for the earrings," Sissy said and showed off the jewelry hanging from her lobes. "I love them."

"My pleasure," Marnie said. "I have a little something else for you, too," she said and pulled an electronic tablet from her tote. The girls were silent as she switched on the device and within seconds, the screen was filled with a friendly face of a woman.

"Hi, there, Sissy," the woman said, waving and smiling. "This is Shay Logan. I just wanted to wish you a wonderful birthday. I know you're spending it with your family and friends and I'm sure you're having a wonderful time. I would have loved to have been there to sing 'Happy Birthday' to you in person. Enjoy your day. Stay awesome. Bye for now!"

The video ended and Joss saw excited tears in his daughter's eyes. "OMG, Shay Logan sent me a birthday message! Did you see that? Dad, did you see it?"

"I saw it, honey," he replied and held Marnie's gaze, mouthing a silent thank-you. She'd asked him about it, of course, making sure he approved of the idea. And had sent him the link to his phone the day before. He knew how excited Sissy would be to receive the message—how much it would mean to her.

She was looking at him, their visual connection so intense it knocked his kneecaps together. Was this what it felt like? Falling for someone. He couldn't remember. Couldn't think with his mind racing so fast. All he knew, to the depths of his soul, was that Marnie Jackson had worked her way into his life... and his heart.

And he was done for.

Chapter Nine

Marnie knew how much the video message meant to Sissy. When she'd asked Shay to do it, her cousin had agreed without a second thought. Shay was one of those entertainers who were always available for their fans. And Sissy's delight was infectious—particularly when she replayed the message for her friends and the rest of the family.

But despite how lovely it was to see Sissy having such a wonderful day, Marnie had been on edge from the moment she arrived. Particularly after talking to Abby, who'd informed her in an offhanded way that her grandmother would be dropping by a little later after her bridge tournament in Rapid City. It was after one o'clock when Marnie noticed Abby talking to a tall and elegant-looking older woman—and then instantly recognized Patience Reed.

The memory of her own mother rushed forward and she saw the similarities—the same chin, the same slanted brows, the same slender shoulders. She wanted to run away and announce her connection at the same time. But she did neither. Instead, she walked up to both women and calmly introduced herself.

"It's lovely to meet you," Patience said and shook her hand. "My great-grandson said he really enjoyed his first class with you this week."

Marnie wanted desperately to feel something—anything—a link, a sign that her grandmother felt something when their hands touched. But there wasn't so much as a flicker in the older woman's light blue eyes.

"T.J. is a wonderful student and a great help in the class," Marnie said, holding on to her nerves, even though they were at fraying point. "I feel very fortunate to be at such a good school."

"Gran volunteers with reading in the kindergarten class," Abby supplied and then sighed. "I wish I had more time to volunteer."

Marnie's head reeled. For so long she'd imagined the moment she would meet her grandmother. She'd imagined what she would say—how she would talk about her mother and ask Patience why she'd given her child up for adoption. If she'd ever tried to find her child. If she would have welcomed her back into her life. There were so many questions and she wondered when or if she'd ever get the opportunity to ask them.

"My granddaughter is too modest. Did you know she volunteers with cooking classes down at the local veterans' home every month?"

It wasn't really a question, Marnie thought as she watched the interaction between the two women. They clearly had a tight-knit bond, one that was enviable, and she was suddenly filled with a yearning and longing for *family*. Her throat ached from the rawness of words unsaid. Her heart hurt from the way it pounded behind her ribs. She had her own family back in Bakersfield. She had her aunt and her cousins, particularly Shay. She even had her father. But in that moment, she wanted more. She wanted to be included in the affection she witnessed between the two women in front of her. She wanted the family her own mother had been denied.

But now wasn't the time. She had to find a way to confront Patience, and that way was not at a teenager's birthday party. She excused herself, feeling the sting of tears burning her eyes, and headed for the house. She found the bathroom on the ground floor and spent a few minutes tidying herself up, dabbing at her red-rimmed eyes and swallowing the rawness in her throat. When she walked back down the hallway, she spotted Joss standing at the bottom of the stairs.

"Everything okay?" he asked, his expression narrowed. "You took off pretty quickly from the barn."

"Nature called," she said and sighed. "This house is amazing," she said, shifting the subject.

"Have you been upstairs?" he asked and when she shook her head, he held out his hand. "Come on, I'll give you the ten-cent tour."

Marnie took his hand and his fingers entwined with hers. They were halfway up the stairs when he stopped and drew her attention to one of the photographs on the wall.

"That's my mother, Louise," he said, gesturing to a pretty woman in her thirties who was wearing a short floral dress and flat shoes.

A man had his arm loped affectionately across her shoulders. "Is that your dad?"

"Yeah. Billie-Jack."

Marnie met his gaze. He looked a little lost—and she knew that feeling all too well. And suddenly, she wanted to talk—really talk. She wanted to share thoughts and feelings. But she couldn't tell him anything about herself. Instead, she grasped on to another subject. "Would you tell me about the accident?"

He regarded her curiously. "The accident?"

"The one where your brother nearly died," she clarified. "What happened?"

He looked at the photo again, then back to her,

and he let out a long sigh. "The old man had been drinking late the night before, and that morning he was more unbearable than usual. It was a Saturday and Mitch was already out, delivering a couple of head of cattle to one of the local ranchers. Billie-Jack started on at me about something and I remember telling him to take a hike. He had the strap he used to keep above the kitchen door in his hand within seconds and I knew I was in for a walloping." He urged her up a couple more steps. "Jake intervened, as he always did, to take the heat off the rest of us and the two of them threw a few punches."

They were on the landing now, looking down at the wide stairway. "Then what happened?"

"I took off for my room and locked the door. I heard Billie-Jack yelling to Grant and Hank to get into the truck. And Grant was just a kid, so he did what he was told. And Hank, he always tried to be the peacemaker, you know…kind of makes sense that he went into law enforcement as a career."

Despite there being a party outside, the house was eerily quiet. "Tell me the rest."

The pressure of his fingers increased a little. "Billie-Jack took off and Jake followed on his motorcycle. The truck crashed and thankfully Grant was thrown free. Hank was stuck inside and the old man didn't try and get him out."

"That's how your brother got the scar on his face?" she asked quietly.

He nodded. "And he suffered burns to thirty per-cent of his body. It was a long and painful recovery."

"And your father?"

"He took off a few weeks later," he replied emo-tionlessly. "Did us all a favor."

Marnie noticed the way the pulse throbbed in his jaw. "I sense a 'but' in there somewhere."

He shrugged his beautiful shoulders. "Maybe if I hadn't told the old man to take a hike, it wouldn't have happened."

Marnie was silent. She saw the guilt in his ex-pression and her heart lurched for him. "You don't believe that, do you?"

He shrugged again. "I don't know. Maybe."

"Have you said anything to your brother?"

His gaze sharpened for a second and he exhaled heavily. "I've never said that to anyone except my wife. She had the same look you do right now."

"She was a wise woman."

"That she was," he said and slowly brought her knuckles to his mouth, kissing her softly. "Wanna see my old room?"

Marnie smiled. "Sure."

He walked up the hallway and entered a room on the left. It was decked out with bunk beds, and styled in various shades of pink and purple, with a picture of a unicorn on the wall. There was even a fluffy cushion on the chair near the window.

She raised a quizzical brow. "Really?"

"The girls decorated it." He grinned. "I did say it was my *old* room. They use this when they stay at the ranch. The master suite is down there," he said and pointed to a door on the right. "Then there are two other guest rooms and the nursery."

"Are your brother and Tess planning on having more children?"

He shrugged. "They had a hard time having a baby—Charlie is something of a miracle—so I'm not sure if they'll try for another."

"Do you want more kids?"

Whoa, girl...could you be any more obvious?

But being so close to him, her ovaries were doing all kinds of things.

"Maybe," he said and then shrugged one shoulder. "I mean, I love the girls, I'm sure I'd feel the same about any other kids I have."

"Well, now that you're the father of a teenager, you'll have a ready-made babysitter," she teased.

He winced. "Don't remind me. I feel old."

Marnie laughed softly. "Wait until she starts dating… That's sure to age you."

"You know, you're not the least bit funny," he replied. "And Sissy isn't allowed to date until she's at least eighteen."

"Weren't you married with a baby on the way at eighteen?" she reminded him and leaned back a little on the doorjamb.

"Precisely."

Marnie looked up at him as he closed the gap between them. "You planning on kissing me?"

"I think so," he replied. "Is that okay?"

"You know," she said and rested her free hand against his chest. "At some point kissing isn't going to be enough, right?"

He nodded. "It's already not enough. But I'm leaving that up to you."

Marnie's heart hammered. "Giving me all the power?"

"Absolutely," he said and chuckled as his mouth came down on hers in a way that was sinfully erotic and mind-blowingly sensual.

She wasn't sure how long they stayed like that, in the doorway, just kissing, just mouths fused together in a way that could almost be G-rated, except for the thrum of desire she knew was coursing through them both.

"Ah—guys," an unexpected voice said and they instantly sprang apart. "Ever heard the expression, get a room?"

They turned and spotted Ellie striding down the hall, grinning broadly as she passed them and headed for one of the guest rooms.

"Busted," Joss said and chuckled. "Sorry about that."

Marnie ran a hand over her hair. "Just as much my fault as yours," she muttered.

It took about ten seconds for them to head downstairs and return to the party. By late afternoon, most of the guests had left and only the family and a few friends remained. They'd moved the celebration to the house, and a buffet of snacks was laid out on a table in the living room. Despite the turmoil of meeting her grandmother, and of getting busted making out with Joss, Marnie was oddly relaxed. She enjoyed the comradery and solidarity of the Culhanes. They loved one another fiercely and clearly had one another's back. Again, it made her long for her own kin.

"That's the same look you had on your face a couple of hours ago when you raced off from the barn," Joss said as he came up behind her, resting a hand gently on her shoulder. "Everything okay?"

"I'm fine," she assured him. "I promise. Just feeling a little homesick, that's all."

"Natural," he said. "Anything I can do to help you with that?"

Hold me, she longed to say, desperately wanting to rest back against him and feel his strong arms around her. "Be my friend," she said quietly.

His head came a little closer. "That's all?"

"No," she replied. "But I'm trying to keep a level head and not fall for you."

"Would that be so bad?"

"That's a loaded question," she flipped back. "I could ask you the same thing."

"So, ask me," he dared.

Marnie turned a little. "If I fall for you, will you break my heart?"

"Not intentionally," he replied. "I try to live my life honestly. Don't you?"

Guilt pressed down on her shoulders. Because she wasn't honest—not by a long shot.

And somehow, she sensed that Joss knew it.

Joss usually got roped into playing the piano when there was a family gathering at the Triple C. Christmas, Thanksgiving, birthdays—it was something of a tradition. But he'd never played in front of someone he was dating. Lara, of course, used to sing along, even though she could barely hold a tune. Playing in front of Marnie, though, filled him with an almost overwhelming performance anxiety. And he also got the sense that all his brothers knew it.

Afterward, he steered clear of her for a while, trying to work out in his head what was going on. Lots of talk, for starters. And kissing—which was great—but also as frustrating as hell.

"I feel inadequate," she said when she finally sidled up beside him next to the piano, while a final round of coffee was being served by Tess and Mrs. B.

"Why's that?"

"Are you kidding?" she replied. "The girls said you could play the piano—but I wasn't expecting that. You're amazing."

"Yeah, my one talent," he said and then raised a brow. "Well, maybe not just that."

"So," she said, looking down at the floor, "are we still on for next weekend?"

"For sure. The girls will be in Rapid City. I'm all yours."

They both knew what it meant. There was no innuendo. No hinting. Just plain old fact. They were going to sleep together the following weekend and change the dynamic of their relationship. After avoiding the obvious, Joss accepted what was happening—they were dating.

And of course, in true torturous style, the week dragged by slowly. By Thursday he was so wound up he could barely think straight. He saw her a couple of times for dinner with the girls. Even though he knew she had classes to plan and papers to grade, she was very generous with her time. She helped Sissy with a history assignment one afternoon, and then she spent time with Clare, teaching her more cupcake recipes. She had so easily merged into their lives, and Joss was amazed at how his daughters had grown to love her so quickly. He'd dropped Marnie's car off in the afternoon and made plans to see her the following evening when he returned from Rapid City.

"Dad," Clare said on the drive to Rapid City. "Is Marnie your girlfriend now?"

"Of course she is," Sissy said and tutted. "Or she would be if he had any sense."

Joss scowled at his eldest daughter. "All right, lighten up, will you?"

"Is she gonna move in with us?" Clare asked, relentless.

"No," he said quickly. "Of course not."

"Nana and Pop always ask if you've got a girlfriend," Clare said and frowned. "What do we tell them now?"

"Nothing," he replied. "Marnie and I are just friends for now. If that changes, I'll tell your grandparents myself."

"They miss Mommy," Clare said softly.

"So do I," he said. "We all miss her."

"I'd miss Marnie, too, if she left," Clare said.

She is leaving...in five months and one week.

"Try not to screw this up, Dad," Sissy said when they got out of the car outside their grandparents' house. "We like Marnie...and as much as we love you, Dad, it would be nice to have a woman in the house to talk to for a change."

He knew they longed for female company...knew they wanted a mother to call their own. And with everything that he was, Joss wished he could give them what they wanted.

"I'll try not to do anything stupid," he assured them.

He said goodbye to his daughters and drove back to Cedar River, stopping by Jo-Jo's on the way home to pick up a pizza, and was at Marnie's by seven. She greeted him at the door with a kiss and a smile, looking lovely in a long, pale blue dress that had a row of tiny buttons down the front. He'd seen her in the dress before, and loved how it flared over her hips, accentuating her womanly shape. He wondered, for a fleeting moment, how he'd ever considered her anything other than beautiful. Her hair bounced around her shoulders as she moved. Her skin was smooth and supple, her blue eyes sparkling bright and clear, and a heady surge of attraction rumbled through his blood. Ten minutes later they were in the kitchen sharing pizza and a bottle of wine.

"Clare asked me if you were my girlfriend," he said.

She held the pizza slice midair. "And what did you say?"

"I didn't get much of chance to say anything. Sissy told me not to screw it up."

Marnie's mouth curved into a smile. "Don't you just love having daughters."

"Usually," he replied. "Not so much when they're smarter than me."

"What do you mean?" she asked, clearly knowing exactly what he meant.

Joss reached across and grasped her hand. "They like you a lot. They want you in their life."

"I like them, too," she admitted and twirled her fingers into his palm. "You, on the other hand…"

"You mean, when liking is more than liking?

Yeah," he said and let out a breath. "That's when it's tough."

Her touch was like an electric current and at the same time like tonic, as though it could cure all his ails. *Balm for the soul.* He remembered Mitch saying that once to him, about Tess. He'd joked about it at the time, calling his brother sentimental… Now he began to understand. There was something curative about Marnie…a soft, gentle spirit that was undeniably magnetic. He'd felt it from the first, those few short weeks ago. At the time he'd resisted and almost resented the sensation…now, he longed for it like a thirsty man craved water.

"It's mutual, you know," she admitted.

Joss nodded. "I know."

"I'm not sure how it all happened so fast."

"Does time matter?"

She shrugged. "Usually—but there's nothing *usual* about how I'm feeling. So, are you going to spend the night?" she asked quietly, almost hesitantly.

Joss's gut plummeted. God, he wanted to, so much. "Am I invited?"

"Yes."

He knew she was giving him an option—knew she understood how much, for him, there was at stake. It was one more reason to want her. When someone else might have shrugged off his concerns, Marnie was too intuitive not to notice he was drowning under the weight of needing to do the right thing for his family, his kids and for them both.

"Do you need promises?" he asked quietly. "Assurances?"

"Usually, yes," she replied. "But not right now. I just want to be with you."

Her bedroom was the furthest one down the hall. Not the largest, but the one with the view of the yard and the flowering hedge. She'd bought new linens, and the beige-and-white palette seemed to add space to the room. She held his hand and lingered in the doorway for a moment.

"I haven't done this in a while," she admitted.

"Me, either."

"I haven't done this all that much, I guess I mean."

Joss pulled her close, feeling her curves against him. "I wish I could say the same thing. But the truth is, I've only had real feelings for one woman in my life, until now. And I'm not quite sure what to do with those feelings."

"Do this," she said huskily, and pressed closer and reached around to run her hands through his hair. "I've been wanting to do that since the first time I met you," she admitted.

Joss kissed her slowly, lingering because he knew that was what she liked. Her hands were on his chest, her breasts pressed against him and it sent his libido skyrocketing. There was a lamp on the bedside table and the light was enough to create shadows on the wall. She pulled back and put some distance between them and then slowly began undoing the row of buttons.

"I'm glad you're doing that," he admitted and chuckled. "I was thinking about how I'd get them undone without snapping the buttons."

"You've been thinking about my buttons?"

"Every time I see you in that dress," he admitted and smiled, watching as the fabric fell apart and the dress slipped off her shoulders. She wore black lace underwear—the sexy, R-rated kind that were the stuff of fantasies, and he ached to touch her through the lace fabric. "You are so beautiful."

She looked away for a moment, like his words embarrassed her, and then she met his gaze straight on. "I've never worn this before."

Joss looked to where her breasts almost spilled over the top of the bra. "Well, I'm glad you're wearing it now."

She laughed and he liked that the mood between them was like that—not too serious.

He flipped off his boots and socks and stripped out of his shirt, watching as she pulled back the duvet and lay on the bed, looking more provocative than he'd ever imagined. He swallowed hard, felt all the blood rush to the lower half of his anatomy and figured he'd have trouble getting out of his jeans if he kept looking at her. But looking elsewhere was impossible. He sat on the bed and traced a long finger from her throat and down her chest and over her rib cage. She shivered and arched her back and he leaned in to kiss her. It wasn't like before, when they'd both shown restraint. There was no one to interrupt, no boundaries to worry about, nothing to keep them apart.

Her hands were instantly at his shoulders, her tongue in his mouth, her breath mingling with his in a way that was mind-blowing. They kissed over and over and then he trailed down, pausing between her breasts and the creamy flesh that tipped over the bra. He kissed her there, cupping her, rubbing his thumb over a straining nipple. She moaned and the sound reverberated in his chest, clanging at his heart. He wasn't sure how long they kissed for, how long they touched, but it would never be long enough, he realized.

He stripped off her underwear and touched her intimately. There wasn't anything shy or reserved about her response. She knew what she wanted, she asked for it, uttering words against his mouth that were so damned erotic he could barely draw in more than one ragged breath at a time. Her hands were at his belt, impatient almost, pulling the leather through the loops before she undid the snap on his jeans.

"Take them off," she demanded, smiling in a way that almost sent him over the edge. "I've wanted to see you naked since the first night I met you."

He chuckled at her admission and did as she

asked, quickly extracting the condom he had in his wallet. She unclipped the bra and as her breasts surged forward he sucked in a breath. He cupped one breast, and then the other, feeling the weight of them in his hands and then gently stroked the nipples with his thumbs. She groaned, low and raspy, in her throat, and finally they were both naked, lying chest to breast, hip to hip. He kissed her again, anchoring her head gently, taking and giving, finding her tongue over and over.

"Marnie," he whispered against her mouth, tasting her lips. "You take my breath away."

She smiled against his mouth. "I think that's the loveliest thing anyone has ever said to me."

Joss quickly had the condom in place and moved over her, resting his weight on his forearms. "Okay?"

"More than okay," she assured him. "Everything I want."

Everything I need...

That was all he could think as he moved inside her, as he felt her body so wondrous beneath him. She was all curves and soft skin, the cradle of her thighs made for him, he thought, finding peace and solace amid the desire that thrummed through him. Perfect harmony. A calm and perfect union. It had been years since he'd experienced such an intimate connection to another human being. The memory of all those one-night stands suddenly faded until all he saw was Marnie, her glittering blue eyes linked to his, her body moving with his in perfect unison.

Her hands were in his hair, then on his back, his hips, urging him closer, deeper, and they created an erotic rhythm that set his skin on fire. She said his name, arching her back as pleasure overtook her and he watched in wonder as she came apart, joining her moments later in a white-hot surge of release.

When it was over, he could barely draw enough breath into his lungs. He looked down at her, mesmerized by the rosy hue of color on her chest and neck. He kissed her jaw and the tender spot beneath her ear, nuzzling a little, and the action made her giggle.

"That tickles," she whispered, still gripping his hips as she inhaled deeply. "You smell good."

"It's just soap."

"It's nice," she said and sighed. "Everything about this feels so nice."

"Mmm," he agreed. "But I need to get up for a minute."

She nodded and he experienced a sharp and bereft sensation the moment he was up and off the bed. He headed for the bathroom to dispose of the condom and when he returned to her bedroom she was lying on her side, one knee curled up a little, her generous breasts uncovered and the duvet at her feet.

Joss stood in the doorway, still semi aroused and getting more turned on as the seconds ticked by.

"You know, I kind of had you pegged for the shy type."

Her brows rose. "Well, you've seen all of me that there is to see, so there's really no point in being coy, is there?"

He laughed. "I guess not."

"But you're right," she said as she looked him up and down and without any modesty or regret. "I am usually modest and shy. But not with you. I don't know why," she admitted and shrugged. "Are you coming back to bed?"

"Absolutely," he replied.

"Good," she said, "because I think I want to do that again."

She was a spontaneous and enthusiastic lover. He liked that about her. *He loved that about her.* Whoa... where did that come from? He'd only known her a few weeks. People didn't fall for someone in a matter of weeks. At least, he didn't. He was cautious in relationships. In everything, really. He made good decisions. He didn't take risks. He worked hard, played safe, did the right thing by his kids and the people he cared about.

But as he joined her on the bed, Joss knew he was all out of excuses.

Chapter Ten

Marnie had one plan when she'd moved to Cedar River. And that didn't include falling in love.

But she knew, without a doubt, that she was head over heels in love with Joss.

It was different from how she'd felt about Heath. From her college boyfriend. Different from anything she'd experienced before. There was no angst, no resistance, no self-doubt. She simply loved him. It didn't matter that they'd only known each other for a short time. It didn't matter that she hadn't told him the real reason why she was in Cedar River. All that mattered were the feelings in her heart. Making love with him had confirmed what she'd been suspecting all week.

"Everything okay?"

It was late, well after eleven, and they'd dozed for a bit after a long and erotic marathon session of touching and tasting and doing a whole lot of things she knew were now imprinted in her memory. With Joss, she had no self-doubt, no body image issues, no concerns about being beautiful enough, or thin enough or sexy enough. He was an incredibly generous lover and she couldn't get enough of touching him.

She rolled in his embrace, running a hand up his chest. "Perfect. And not sleepy, which is odd since I've expended more energy in the last couple of hours than I have since forever. You may have noticed that I'm not exactly the sporty type. I do like walking, but since it's been snowing I haven't—"

He laughed. "I love that you talk a lot."

Marnie looked at him, her throat tightening. "You do?"

"It's very endearing," he said and kissed her softly.

So, he didn't just say he loved her, did he? No… impossible. She was reading way too much into the words and quickly changed the subject. "I think I want a cup of tea."

"Good idea."

Fifteen minutes later they were sitting on the sofa, Joss in his jeans and she in an old college T-shirt that came just below her bottom. The heater was on and the room was toasty warm. She sat close to him, her legs curled up, twirling her fingertips through the hair on his chest, thinking how it was the loveliest way to spend the evening. Or morning, since it was just after midnight.

"It's your birthday," he said, almost reading her mind. He sprang up and walked out of the room for a moment, grabbed his jacket from the hall stand, returned to the sofa and quickly resumed his position. "Happy birthday," he said, passing her a wrapped gift.

She could tell it was a book and unwrapped the paper to find a small, red clothbound first edition of a book about Wild Bill. "It's wonderful," she said, inhaling the scent only old books had.

"I figured, what better thing to get a history professor who's just moved to the Black Hills than an old book about Wild Bill Hickock."

"How did you know I collect old books?"

"I...assumed," he said.

"That I'm a book nerd?" she said and smiled, her throat tightening. No one had ever spent the time to get to know her before this, she realized, thinking how Heath had bought her a necklace for her last birthday—jewelry she had never worn. "Guilty as charged. It's lovely, thank you. I am a bona fide book nerd and proud of it."

"You should be," he said. "I hope my daughters grow up to be as successful and independent as you, Marnie. You're a fabulous role model."

"Do you think? Sometimes I feel like a complete fraud. I've learnt languages I never speak, from countries I've never been to. I can cook but rarely do anything more than a noodle cup for dinner because I live alone. I left a perfectly great career in California to come here to teach elementary school because I was looking for…for…" Her words trailed off.

"A new life?" he prompted.

God, if only it were that simple. "I was looking for answers."

"Have you found them?"

Marnie swallowed the lump in her throat. "Yes, I think I have."

His arms moved around her. "Then, maybe it was the right decision."

"Joss…have you ever needed to just find yourself?" she asked and then shook her head. "My guess is you've always known who you are and what you should be doing, and I imagine that with losing your wife so young and with two kids, you needed to be in control of who you are every single day, correct?"

"Something like that. But I've made mistakes. Hurt people without intending to. The good thing about life, Marnie, is we all get a do-over."

"My mom didn't," she said and dropped her head to his shoulder.

He pointed to a picture on the sideboard. "That's your mom?"

"Yeah. She suffered with bipolar disorder and

there were times when she was so hard to love, hard to be around, even…but I stuck with her because I loved her."

"There were bad times?" he asked gently.

She nodded. "Yeah…days of silences. Days of her laying in bed. Days of her not eating, just sleeping, just blocking out a world she found so hard to be a part of."

"That must have been difficult for you to watch," he said, tracing tiny circles on her back with his fingertips.

"It was," she admitted, her heart aching as the memories flowed. "I'd sit outside her door and talk for hours, just trying to break the silence, you know. I do that a lot," she said and sighed. "I mean, talk a lot. It's my go-to response when I feel like I'm out of my comfort zone, or when someone is quiet."

He nodded, like he knew exactly why she sometimes chatted on. "That's not a bad thing, though. It means you're caring and trying to fill in the gaps."

Marnie shuddered. "I'm not sure my mom ever saw it that way. You know, when she was on a high, she was amazing. I think I told you she was adopted," she said quietly, trying to find the words she needed. "Well, a few months before she died, she finally found her birth mother's identity. She'd been looking for so long and wanted to put the pieces together. But then she got sick and died not long after. She had a cut on her leg and it got infected and the infection attacked her heart and her immune system couldn't fight it. She was gone in a matter of a week. Her fever got so high she slipped into a coma. I didn't even get the chance to say goodbye. Afterward, I felt so guilty that she never got to finish her journey."

"But you can't live that journey for her," he said gently.

"I can try," she replied and closed her eyes wearily, feeling his nearness wrap around her like a cloak.

They headed back to bed shortly after and when she awoke it was a little after six. There was light beaming through the crack in the curtains and she reached out for Joss, only to find the sheets cold beside her. For a fleeting moment, she wondered if she'd imagined their night together. But then she saw his shirt hanging over the chair near the window and sighed with relief. Her body ached with an unusual but not altogether unpleasant lethargy, and when she dragged herself out of bed she was smiling. She could smell coffee and followed the scent to the kitchen.

And there he was, standing behind the counter in his jeans, the top button undone, his glorious physique all hers to ogle even at the crack of dawn. She spent a few seconds admiring him and then cleared her throat.

He turned instantly. "Hey, birthday girl."

Had she ever woken to a lovelier birthday? It was

so easy being with him that she didn't question it, didn't dwell on how long their *thing* would last. Because it felt right. Instead, she walked further into the kitchen and kissed him.

Joss had made the arrangements to give Marnie the second part of her birthday gift—a horse ride at the Triple C—and was delighted by her excitement. She was dressed in the right gear, from jeans to a pair of Sissy's cowboy boots that easily fit her, and was now standing beside her mount, an aged liver chestnut mare named Pepper, who had had more than her fair share of novice riders and beginners on her back over the years.

"She's so beautiful," Marnie said and patted the mare's neck.

"You ready?" he asked and came up behind her.

She nodded. "For sure."

He helped her into the saddle and then spent half an hour with her in the corral. Thankful that his brother and sister had given him some alone time, even though he suspected they were watching from the house. Once he was confident she had the reins under control, he clipped on a lead and mounted his sister's horse, Valiant, and headed off. There were several riding trails on the ranch and he took the shortest one, since it was her first time in the saddle. But he watched the way she moved with the horse and realized she was a natural.

"Having fun?" he asked, keeping the horses to a gentle amble.

"Amazing," she said. "One thing off my bucket list."

Joss eased Valiant back a little. "What else is on your list?"

"I want to go to Paris and walk along the Champs-Élysées, and then go to Venice and ride in a gondola," she supplied. "And I want to see the aurora borealis. And I want to have the courage to skydive. I'd like to try colored contact lenses. And of course I'd like to get married and have a couple of babies one day."

It didn't seem like such an outrageous list—and some of the things he could certainly help her with!

"I think all those things are achievable," he remarked, not looking at her for fear she'd see the truth in his eyes. That he *could* give her those things. That they could share them—together. That they could be a family.

"I hope so," she said. "What about you?"

He shrugged. "I guess I'd like to travel a little. I'm not sure about the skydiving thing. And I think I could handle another baby or two—I'm an expert diaper changer."

"I suppose you'd like a son?"

"Yeah," he said and looked at her, imagining a little boy with his hair and her eyes. "I think I would."

She was quiet for a while after that, enjoying the ride, the horses, the wide-open space of the ranch.

Joss hadn't been out pleasure-riding for a long time and didn't realize how much he'd missed it. They stayed out for a couple of hours, taking a break near the creek, drinking from the water bottles he'd stored in the saddlebag. They tethered the horses up and sat on an old tree stump.

"It's so beautiful here. I can't imagine what it must feel like knowing you're a part of something so expansive, so vast. I grew up living in a small brick-and-tile bungalow in suburbia. But this—" she opened up her arms expressively "—it's spectacular. You can trace your family back here how many generations?"

"Five," he replied.

"I envy you."

He didn't respond, didn't know what to say to her earnest words. She was so effortlessly open, and the more time he spent with her, the more he wanted to be with her. And of course he recognized that for what it was—he might be a guy, it might have been years since he'd had the feeling, but he knew what falling in love felt like.

She moved sideways a little and pressed against him and it was all the invitation he needed to kiss her. They made out for a while, just kissing, just getting to know each other a little more. Her hands were on his chest, in that spot over his heart, and he wondered if she knew she did that. When they finally dragged their lips apart, she was panting, her blue eyes luminous in her face, her cheeks flushed with a heady glow, her mouth full of temptation. He thought then, a sharp sensation that arrowed deep down in his belly, that her mouth was the one he wanted to kiss for the rest of his life.

But what could he say? *Don't leave Cedar River in five months. Don't let my kids love you and then walk away. Don't let* me *love you and then walk away.*

Joss got to his feet and suggested they get back. The return ride took over an hour, most of which they did with him keeping silent, just listening as she talked, hearing the whimsy in her voice as she absorbed their surroundings. When they got back to the barn, one of the young ranch hands greeted them and took the horses to remove the gear and brush them down. She gave Pepper a lingering pat and promised to come back and see her again.

"So," he said as they walked toward the house, "what do you think?"

"I loved it," she replied and then winced. "Although I think my thighs will be feeling it for the next few days. Could be a combination of things, though," she added and gave him a long, flirty look that almost dropped him to his knees.

Joss draped a companionable arm over her shoulder. "Jake and Abby are here," he said when he spotted their car.

Did he feel her stiffen? He couldn't be sure. It

seemed an odd response since he was sure she liked his brother and his wife.

"Great," she said after a moment.

They were all in the kitchen, and no one raised so much as a brow when they entered the room. One thing about his family, they were good at letting people into their lives.

Except Billie-Jack.

Which wasn't the same thing, because he wanted to come *back* into their lives and there was too much damage done in the past for that to ever happen, he was certain of it.

She was standing beside Abby, who was wishing her a happy birthday, when Ellie spoke.

"You know," his sister said in her usual matter-of-fact way, "except for the hair color, you two look really alike... You could almost be sisters."

Joss glanced their way and realized his sister was right. Both women shared a similar jawline and cheekbones, and their eyes were the same bright blue. Marnie was fuller-figured and Abby a little taller, but there was no denying the similarities.

She met his gaze and smiled, almost warily, he thought, as though the idea unnerved her. She probably wasn't used to such a large and robust family dynamic. From what she'd said, there was mostly her mother and her aunt and a couple of cousins. Her absent father didn't make the grade. It was something they had in common.

Joss moved forward and reached for her hand, gently urging her closer. He didn't care what his family would make of the action. Most of them had been busting his balls for years, telling him to find someone again. So, now he had, and he had the sudden and inexplicable urge to protect her from their combined curiosity.

They left shortly after and she seemed relieved. He didn't ask why. Part of him didn't want to know. He wanted her to like his family. He wanted her to be a part of them. He dropped her at home and then headed back to his own place to get cleaned up and changed. He knew they had to talk; he just didn't know what to say. It was too early for any declaration, any questions, any promises. But he didn't want her to think he wasn't invested, either. He had a history of no commitment…so he understood if she had reservations.

When he returned to her house he lingered on the porch for a moment and then tapped on the door. Of course, he had a key, but it was Marnie's home and he would never overstep the boundaries. She opened the door quickly and invited him inside. She'd changed into a short pale green dress and all he could think was how he wanted to get her out of it. Which didn't take long, because the moment he crossed the threshold she grasped his forearm and pulled him close.

They spent most of the afternoon in her bed,

making leisurely love, and it was nearly five thirty when they roused. "You know," he said and ran a hand down her back. "I made dinner reservations at O'Sullivan's for tonight."

She wrinkled her nose. "Couldn't we go and get pizza and come back and watch a movie instead?"

"Really? You'd prefer to go to JoJo's pizza parlor than a swanky hotel?"

She nodded. "I don't feel like getting dressed up. To be honest, I'd much rather get pizza and then come back here and get back into bed."

Joss chuckled. "Well, it is your birthday, after all, and you should get what you want."

That settled, he canceled the reservation and around six fifteen they headed to JoJo's. Joss had known the owner, Nicola, since high school and he waved to her as they entered the restaurant. They weren't exactly friends, but they were friendly, and she quickly showed them to one of the booth seats. He was surprised to see Hank and Ellie arrive a few minutes later, with his nephew T.J. His siblings made a beeline across the room for them.

"I thought you guys were heading to O'Sullivan's?" Ellie queried when she reached their table.

"My fault," Marnie said and shrugged. "I wanted pizza. Are you joining us?"

Joss's gut sank. He really didn't want to deal with relatives, but he knew he didn't have any choice when they slid into the booth across from them, T.J. between them.

"Patience is here, too," Ellie said and didn't look the least bit apologetic for interrupting their evening. At least Hank had the sense to mutter an apology for intruding on their date. "Jake and Abby have some art show thing in Rapid City tonight," Ellie said and smiled. "We just bumped into Patience outside and thought we'd all have pizza."

"Patience is coming?" Marnie asked, her voice tighter than usual.

"She's parking her car. This one wouldn't let her park in the loading zone outside," Ellie said and jerked a disagreeable thumb in Hank's direction.

"It's illegal to park in a loading zone," Hank persisted.

"Blah-blah-blah," Ellie said with a smile and waved a hand. "So, are you guys actually dating, or what?"

Only Ellie would ask such a blunt and to-the-point question. And get away with it. "Behave yourself, sis," Joss warned gently and didn't answer the question.

"Who, me?" Ellie said and her smile widened.

Patience joined them soon after and squeezed in beside Marnie. They ordered bread for starters, a couple of pizzas, alcohol-free mojitos and a lime soda for T.J., who was watching them all with keen interest.

"You know, Miss Jackson," the youngster said, looking directly at Marnie, and using her name formally because he was used to that at school. "You have exactly the same color eyes as my mom… like *exactly*," he emphasized. "And the same color as Great-Gran," he said after a little more musing. "That's weird."

Joss felt Marnie stiffen beside him and he reached under the table and rested a gentle hand on her thigh. She seemed a little out of sorts and he wondered if all his family crowding around them was too much for her.

"Lots of people have the same color eyes," Joss assured his nephew. "Like us," he said and gestured to the three of them sitting opposite.

T.J., who was very advanced for his age, rolled his eyes dramatically. "That's 'cause we're related, Uncle Joss. And people who are related have lots of things the same as each other."

T.J.'s logic was spot-on, but no one made another comment. Instead, they spent an hour eating pizza and laughing and doing what Joss loved most—being a family. He wished his daughters had been there, too, missing them so much his chest hurt. Once dinner was done, Joss took care of the check and they said their goodbyes.

He grasped Marnie's hand and led her outside and spoke again as they were getting into his truck. "Are you okay? You seem quiet."

She nodded. "I'm fine. Just tired."

"I'll take you home."

She nodded again and the ten-minute drive was mostly done in silence. He pulled up outside her house and she grabbed the handle, speaking before he had a chance to. "I think I need to call it a night. Thank you for the lovely day. I'll treasure it always."

Joss reached out and grasped her hand, bringing it to his lips. "Are you sure you're all right?"

"Fine, I promise. But it's been a big day and I think I need to get some sleep."

As far as brush-offs went, it was pretty mild, but he felt the sting of it, and was still feeling it when he got home and wandered around the house, looking for something to keep him occupied during his solitude. He wasn't averse to his own company, but he hadn't expected to be spending the night alone. When the girls were home, he was on point as a parent, but when they went to their grandparents', he got to be a single guy for a couple of days. He hung out with his family, or went to Rusty's with a friend. After the last twenty-four hours, he'd anticipated that he'd be spending his Saturday night in Marnie's bed. Instead, he was alone. He replayed the day in his head, looking for anything that might have had her backpedaling, but nothing came to mind. Maybe she really was just tired? Whatever the reason, he knew he had to stop moping around like a lovesick idiot.

Or he was gonna be screwed.

* * *

Marnie knew that there was going to come a time when she was faced with Patience Reed and would have to confront the other woman with the truth. She sat at her kitchen table and flicked through the papers in front of her—a folder filled with documents and pictures and proof that she was indeed Patience's granddaughter. But of course, the only proof needed was the very obvious physical similarities between herself and Abby and, indeed, Patience herself. Just as Joss's very smart and very inquisitive nephew had pointed out!

She also had to tell Joss the truth before he figured it out and assumed she'd just been playing him the entire time. Either way, she had to talk to him, and had to stop avoiding him like she'd been doing for the past couple of days.

On Tuesday, she got home from school around four and waited to see his truck drive down the street and into his driveway before she headed to his place, a plate of cookies in her hand, the folder tucked in the other. He had the front door open before she made it to the second step.

"Hey, there," he said loosely, but Marnie spotted the tension tightening his shoulders.

"I made cookies," she said and shrugged, lingering on the step. "The ones with the ginger pieces that you like. I called the ranch and Mrs. B gave me the recipe."

Surprise crossed his face. "Just like that? She doesn't give her recipes to just anyone."

Marnie smiled shyly. "I guess I made a good impression."

He hesitated. "Are you coming inside?"

"Marnie, hi!" It was Sissy's voice she heard from behind him and then met his gaze. "Are you staying for dinner?" Sissy asked when she walked to the edge of the top step, and was then joined by Clare, who was clearly delighted to see her, even though they saw one another in class every day. "I'm making tacos. I'm not sure how good they'll turn out," she said and grinned. "But it's gotta be better than Dad's cooking."

"Wicked child," he said.

Marnie's heart was constricting as the seconds passed. "I just came to drop off the cookies," she said and held them out to Sissy. "And talk to your dad for a minute."

She saw his gaze narrow and noticed how he gently nudged Sissy's arm with his elbow, and the two girls offered another beaming smile before they returned inside.

"They're such wonderful kids, Joss," she said.

"They've become very attached to you," he said, a raw edge to his voice. "You know that, right?"

She nodded. "It's mutual."

"Is it?" he queried. "It's difficult to tell with you." And of course, they weren't talking about her attachment to the girls. They were talking about the stagnant state of their relationship.

She pulled on her courage to tell him the truth. "I'm afraid," she admitted in little more than a whisper.

His expression narrowed. "Of me?"

"Of…this," she said and waved a hand between them. "Of falling for you. Of being a part of something that feels so *right*."

"That's why you've mostly ignored me for three days?"

She nodded, heat climbing up her neck. He was right. She *had* ignored him. Dismissed him. Done little more than answer a couple of text messages as briefly as she could. "Yeah."

"It tore me up a bit, you know," he said as he came down the steps and stood in front of her. "And the girls have missed you."

"I've missed them, too."

"You know, I'd never intentionally hurt you."

"Of course, I know that. It's more about me, I think, what I'm afraid of. In the past I've been—"

"That's just it, Marnie, it's not just about you," he said, cutting her off more harshly than she suspected he intended. "It's about you and me and the girls. All of us are invested here. And I know you've been hurt in the past, but *I'm* not a cheater. Not all men do that. If I'm with you, then I'm *with* you. Just you."

"For how long?" she asked, her voice breaking a little.

He shrugged and ran a hand through his hair. "I don't know… You're the one who's only here for six months," he reminded her. "I don't have a timeline. Cedar River is my home. My kids are here, my family is here, my life is here."

Again, he was right. "I just don't know what the future will hold."

"Who does?" he shot back. "I never imagined I'd be a single dad at twenty-three. Or that nearly a decade later I'd meet you. Life is full of surprises. It's what we do with those surprises that counts."

He held out his hand and while she considered hesitating, she didn't, and accepted his touch because it was the most wonderful tonic. The most wonderful feeling she had ever known.

"It's all happened so fast," she said, knowing it was an excuse to pull back. And knowing he knew it.

"It goes both ways," he said. "But we can slow down, if that's what you want. I'm not going anywhere."

She was, that was his point. She had a six-month contract and then…what? Back to Bakersfield? Back to her soulless apartment? To her friends and family and to the life that had never truly given her joy? Now that her mom was gone, there was little holding her there. For a flash of a second she imagined another life, a life that included Joss and his kids and the small town at the foot of the Black Hills. She saw them as a real family. And she saw other things, too…like a wedding, and a baby. It was a life she suddenly yearned for so deeply it made her ache inside.

"I'll try harder," she promised.

"Just be yourself, Marnie," he said softly, urging her close until their bodies were touching. "Just be honest, that's all I ask for."

She clutched the folder under her arm, desperate to tell him the truth, torn between knowing he deserved the truth, and her own fear of rejection.

"What's going on in that beautiful head of yours?"

She exhaled heavily. "I wish I could tell you."

He grasped her chin, gently tilting her head. "You can tell me anything."

Not this…

"Just be patient with me, okay."

He kissed her softly. "Like I said, I'm not going anywhere."

Joss asking for the truth was a lot, as it turned out. Even though she spent time with him over the following couple of days and fell a little more in love with him, and his daughters, each time they were together. She had dinner with them Tuesday and Wednesday night. Mrs. Floyd was home and back on deck, so she watched the girls Thursday evening and he took her to O'Sullivan's for dinner. Afterward, back at her house, they had a seriously intense make-out session that had her aching for more. He didn't stay over, even though it was what they both wanted. They had sort of agreed to slow things down a little, and she was quietly relieved. She needed to sort herself out—to work out what she wanted and come clean about her reasons for being in Cedar River. After that—maybe they had a shot at a real relationship. *A future*. She already knew she was completely in love with Joss, and even though he hadn't exactly said the words, she felt his feelings through to her bones.

She didn't have a chance to clear the air, though, because late on Friday afternoon he turned up at the school as she was packing up. There was a PTA meeting that afternoon, and she knew he'd been on the committee and was still active and invested when it came to school matters. That was what he did—invest himself—like he had in them, she suspected, before she'd put the wall up over the last few days.

He looked so good in dark cargos and a pale blue shirt and some kind of aviator jacket that amplified the broadness of his shoulders and strong arms. She smiled when she saw him, wanting to kiss him so much, but the school grounds were not the place for kissing.

"What?" he asked and grinned, correctly interpreting her reaction.

Marnie restacked the folders on her desk. "You look hot, that's all I'm saying."

He laughed. "Sissy is going to stay with a friend

and Clare is having a sleepover at the ranch tomorrow night. Feel like hanging out with me?"

She didn't need time to think. "You bet. So, am I going to have to watch all the single PTA moms fight for your attention this evening?"

He laughed again. "No. Haven't you heard? I'm spoken for."

"People might think teachers and parents shouldn't date."

"I don't care what people think. And you're not *my* teacher," he reminded her. "So no rules are being broken."

I'm the one breaking the rules by not telling you the truth...

She had the folder in her tote on the desk, the one with the reports and pictures and every detail of her mother's adoption. All she had to do was pass it to him. He would know the truth. Then she wouldn't feel as alone as she did.

"By the way," he said and smiled, "you have no idea how sexy you are in that skirt and blouse and those heels...and the killer glasses. It's like Lois Lane or something."

She laughed loudly. "No one's ever called me that. I think I like it, though. Lois was tough and uncompromising and sassy as hell."

"Like you," he said and grinned and then kissed her so hotly her knees actually buckled.

"Goodness, I'm not good for much of anything

when you do that," she admitted. "And I've got a stack of papers to grade tonight once the meeting is over."

"How about you take them home tonight and I promise not to interrupt you all evening. I won't come over and I won't text. You can message me when you're ready for bed so we can say good-night."

She knew that meant they'd be talking on the phone for at least half an hour. "And how am I going to get to sleep after hearing your voice?"

"I'll tell you a bedtime story," he teased, his grin broadening. "Come on, the meeting starts soon."

She hurriedly gathered up all her folders and pushed them into her tote and then followed him from the room. "Sissy told me you are a stickler for punctuality."

"I am. So, how are you getting along here? Enjoying the job?"

"Very much," she replied. "The kids are wonderful and I really feel as though I've settled in well with the faculty. I thought I'd miss teaching young adults, but I don't. The young kids are so willing to learn, almost joyful when something resonates with them. Cynicism comes with age, I suspect."

He didn't disagree. The PTA meeting was being held in the library and they waved to Abby, who was already in attendance. Marnie held on to her nerves when she saw her and took a seat beside a couple of the other teachers, while Joss sat next to his sister-in-law. As far as meetings went, it was pretty run-of-the-mill, with the usual school issues being discussed and several items being held over until the next meeting. When it was over, she spent a few moments talking to the principal, Mrs. Santino, and saw that Joss and Abby were by the refreshments table. The majority of parents had already bailed, so there were only half a dozen or so people left in the room.

Joss smiled when Marnie walked toward them, and she didn't see the chair obstructing her, until she noticed Joss pointing to it just as she tripped. She quickly regained her footing, but wasn't quite nimble enough to hang on to her tote and the folders flew out as the bag hit the ground, papers scattering around her feet. Joss and Abby were immediately in front and helped her pick them up. Then her panic set in.

The folder!

The pictures were spread out on the floor and it took about three seconds for Abby to say something.

"What's this?" the other woman asked sharply, holding one of the photographs.

Marnie sucked in her breath and felt the color leach from her face. She looked at Joss, then Abby, blinking, her throat suddenly raw.

"I wanted to… I mean, I can explain—"

"This is a picture of my grandmother," Abby said, cutting her off, her fingers crinkling the paper.

"Marnie?" Joss said her name, clearly trying to

soothe and understand simultaneously. "What's going on?"

"Explain what?" Abby demanded heatedly. "Why do you have a picture of my grandmother?"

She looked around, saw that people were watching her. Then she swallowed hard, felt the words rise up, and then, somehow, fall from her lips. "Because she's my grandmother, too."

Chapter Eleven

Joss stared at her, trying to digest what she'd said. It didn't make sense. How could Patience Reed be her grandmother? He took a couple of seconds as the truth banged around in his head.

"Your mom?" he said, although he wasn't sure how he found a voice. "This is about your mom?"

She nodded. "Yes."

"What's going on?" Abby demanded. "Joss?"

He looked at both women. Loyalty to his family dragging him one way, his feelings for Marnie dragging him another. And he was so torn.

"I have to talk to Patience before I say anything else," she replied and she picked up the papers and grabbed her belongings, tugging the crinkled picture from Abby's hands. "I'm sorry, I have to go."

He watched her leave the room, staring after her, his heart banging so hard behind his ribs he was certain everyone could hear it. The people still in the room were regarding them curiously and he ignored their intrusive stares. "I should go and talk to her," he said quietly.

"Joss," Abby said firmly. "What's this about? What do you know?"

Nothing. "It's not for me to say. And honestly, I'd only be guessing."

"But you're dating her," Abby reminded him. "Surely you know what's going on here? You must know something."

"Like I said," he reiterated. "I'd only be guessing. It's dark outside—I'll walk you to your car."

Once they were in the parking lot, Abby asked again, "Please, Joss… I can't go home and simply let this go unanswered. I need to know."

"I'll go and talk with her, get her to call you and your grandmother," he said. "That's all I can do."

By the time he got to her place it was after seven. Mrs. Floyd was watching the girls, so he had a little time to find out what was going on and get some answers. He tapped on her door and when she opened it, he knew she'd been crying.

"Can I come in?"

She peered around him. "Is Abby with you?"

"Of course not," he snapped. "Come on, Marnie, we really need to talk. Please let me in."

She stepped aside and he crossed the threshold, waiting for her to close the door. She walked into the living room, sat on the edge of the sofa, and didn't speak until he was sitting opposite her.

"Yes," she said, before he could ask a question. "Patience Reed is my mom's birth mother."

He frowned. "You're sure?"

"Positive."

"How can you be so sure?"

"I hired a private detective to find her," she replied, her hands clasped tightly together. "My mother knew her name and was about to start looking for her when she passed away. I continued the search and found her."

"Just Patience?" he asked, his suspicions amplifying as the seconds ticked past. "Or Abby, too?"

"Both of them—anyone connected to Patience Reed."

Heat crawled up his neck. "You make it sound simple."

She shrugged. "It is."

"Then why keep it a secret?"

"It wasn't a secret," she replied. "It just wasn't anyone's business."

One brow shot up. "Really?"

She shrugged loosely. "I was looking for the right time to approach Patience and tell her."

"And were you looking for the right time to tell me?" he shot back. "Or did you think you could keep it a secret forever?"

"It wasn't a secret," she replied quietly, reiterating her words. "It was personal. Private."

"And what's been going on between us these past weeks hasn't been personal and private?" he asked, annoyance settling in his limbs and climbing across his skin. "Is that what you're saying?"

He watched as she swallowed hard, as though every word was difficult. But he wanted answers. He wanted to know why she'd kept such an important thing from him.

Because you don't matter.

And then the truth wound through him like a serpent, settling in his gut and leaving an acrid taste in his mouth. Joss looked at her, staring deeply into her blue eyes. Wanting…*needing* to know her motives.

"Is this why…" His words trailed off, because he was almost afraid to hear her answer. Then he took a breath, harsher, offering some resilience to his fractured feelings. "Did you get into this thing with us just to get close to Abby, knowing she was my sister-in-law, knowing she was the link to your grandmother?"

The fact she didn't immediately deny it told Joss everything he needed to know.

"No… I mean…yes," she said and waved a hand. "I wasn't thinking, you know. I was—"

"Lying," he said sharply and sprang to his feet. "And manipulating everyone. Including me. And my family. My kids, goddamn it!"

"It wasn't like that," she said and stood. "Yes, Patience is my grandmother and I came to Cedar River to try and meet her, and I don't know…to find out why she didn't keep my mother…to maybe even get to know her a little. This thing between us, that hasn't got anything to do with my wanting to connect with my grandmother."

"I don't believe you," he said, his chest filling with a kind of rage that was manifesting into hurt as the seconds passed. "I'm not sure if anything that comes out of your mouth is the truth."

"Joss, please," she said as she took a step toward him.

He stepped back instinctively. He knew what he wanted to hear. What he needed to hear. Because there was so much at stake. Their relationship. His daughters. The foundation of a family he was imagining would be theirs in the future. But all he saw when he looked at her now was lies and manipulation.

"Can you look at me and tell me honestly that the fact Abby is my sister-in-law had nothing to do with us getting together? That when you found out my name you didn't think it would be an easy way to make the connection to Patience?"

She sucked in a breath. "No…yes…but not with any agenda."

"Oh, come on, Marnie," he said and ran a hand over his face. "You gotta see how bad this looks. That's why you agreed to stay at my house, isn't it? That's why you spent so much time with my kids, why you were so obliging. Baking cakes, helping them with their homework." He laughed humorlessly. "You were looking for an angle, right? A way to meet Abby, and then meet your grandmother. Me and the girls were the perfect conduit for you, weren't we?" He hurt so much as he said the words and he was so angry he could barely stand being in his own skin. "I wonder if you actually had any accommodation booked when you first arrived. Maybe you were hoping you could improvise once your car got wrecked. And there I was—the perfect chump—a uneducated grunt who didn't have the smarts to figure out that you were manipulating everything and everyone!"

"It wasn't like that," she said quickly, her cheeks ablaze. "I don't think you're a grunt. Yes, when you first told me your name, I knew you must have been related to Abby. I wasn't sure how, at first. I knew she was married to Jake, but I didn't have much information about his family. I just figured that—"

"That if the surname was the same, then I'd do, right?" he asked, cutting her off. "Pretend as much as you have to, to get what you want?"

"No," she implored. "That's not who I am. These

past few weeks haven't been about me trying to manipulate anyone, particularly you. We've become really close and that's not me pretending anything."

"You mean sex?" he asked, his voice as hollow as his heart. "All sex does is cloud judgment. You lied to me," he said simply. "Over and over. I've been honest with you since the first moment we met. The truth was all I expected in return—not some BS story about wanting a different life and running away from a cheating ex."

"All of that is true," she said. "The thing with my grandmother was simply the catalyst I needed to make some changes. I did want a new life…and I found it, right here…with…with…"

"With me?" he queried, finishing her sentence. He shook his head. "I don't think so. I think you saw an opportunity and you took it."

She moved forward and grasped his arm. "Joss, I'm sorry. But I can't undo the past few weeks. I can't undo the fact that Patience Reed *is* my grandmother, or the fact that you *are* Abby's brother-in-law. They're just the facts. They're not feelings."

Joss looked to where her hand lay on his arm, felt the heat from her touch like it were a branding iron. He didn't want to hear her talk about feelings. Not hers. Not his. He didn't want her telling him how much she cared about his daughters and how much their relationship meant to her. Or how she hadn't fooled and used him. He was too broken up and angry to hear any more.

He shrugged off her touch and took a couple of steps away from her. "You have a rental agreement to live in this house. And you're Clare's teacher. Other than that, I don't want you anywhere near my kids."

Or me...

She turned chalk-pale. "You don't mean that. The girls—"

"Are my daughters," he reminded her. "So, I get to decide who and what is best for them."

"Joss, can't we talk about this?"

"I'm all talked out," he said flatly. "I told Abby I'd ask you to call her or Patience and sort this out. You do what you have to. As for us—we're done."

With that, he walked out with what little strength he had left.

Marnie had never had a broken heart before. A cracked heart, certainly, from when Heath had cheated on her. When her parents divorced, she'd cried herself silly for weeks. And then, when her mom died, she'd experienced a deep and saddening sense of loss that was profound. But this...it was so different.

"So, have you made contact with your grandmother?"

It was Shay who asked. Shay who was the only person who understood her heartbreak, the only person she could turn to. Shay whom she'd called early Sunday morning after spending the past two nights staring at the ceiling and wondering how she'd managed to make such a mess of things. She hadn't seen or heard from Joss. She hadn't heard from anyone—and that made her feel more alone than she'd imagined possible. So, she'd called the one person whom she trusted completely, because she knew she wouldn't get censured or criticized.

"Not yet," she admitted and held the cell phone to her ear. She didn't want to video chat, didn't want Shay to see her gray pallor or red-rimmed eyes. It was enough that her cousin knew she'd wrecked everything and spent the past thirty-six hours crying. "It all happened so fast and was so intense... I'm not sure how I'll make contact now."

"What about calling this Abby person? Maybe set up a meeting?" Shay suggested.

"Ah, Abby didn't exactly seem thrilled to learn we shared the same grandmother," Marnie replied. "I don't think she's ready to embrace the idea that we're cousins."

"Nonsense," Shay said gently. "She'd be lucky to have you. You're *my* cousin and I adore you."

"You're biased because we've been best friends forever."

Shay laughed. "And how are things with hot single dad?"

"Terrible. I think I've blown it."

"He has to understand you were just trying to protect your grandmother."

"I think he suspects I was simply trying to protect myself," Marnie said and sighed heavily. "And he'd be right. I should have told him about Patience the moment we became… I don't know…more than friends. Now he believes I got involved with him to get closer to my grandmother and cousin. And maybe I did. Maybe I did and I was too much in lust with him to notice. He said sex clouds people's judgment and he was right about that, too."

"Are you in love with him?" Shay asked bluntly.

Marnie inhaled. "I think so… I mean… I…"

"Is he in love with you?"

Her throat burned. "I don't know. I thought he might… I mean, I know he feels something. But right now he's furious because he thinks I lied to him."

"You didn't exactly lie," Shay said encouragingly.

"By omission I did. And I had plenty of opportunity to tell him. But I didn't because I was afraid of losing him, which is precisely what happened, so I was right to be worried."

"So, what are you going to do?" her cousin asked.

"Honestly, I don't know."

"I wish I was there with you," Shay said and sighed.

"Yeah," Marnie said. "Me, too."

When she ended the call, Marnie spent a couple of hours thinking about her predicament. To get her out of her funk, she did some classroom prep for the upcoming week and did some baking. By then she was tired of her wallowing and her own company, so she took a shower, got dressed and headed into town. She needed to do some grocery shopping.

She was wheeling the shopping cart by the fruit and veg section when she heard her name being called. Marnie turned and noticed Ellie standing a few feet away.

"Hey, there," the other woman said.

"Hi," Marnie replied and then noticed the look on Ellie's face. "I guess you've heard."

Ellie's eyes wrinkled up. "News travels fast in my family. How are you holding up?"

Marnie's insides twitched. So, maybe not everyone with the surname Culhane hated her right now. "I'm okay. Kind of numb, I think."

"Everyone's pretty mad at you," Ellie said bluntly.

"Everyone?" she echoed, feeling ill to the pit of her stomach.

"Oh, you know, Joss of course, and Abby. And probably Jake because he's Abby's husband. I'm sure they'll get over it once they've calmed down. We've all done stupid stuff in our life."

Marnie smiled, the first time in days. "I'm not so sure this will be forgotten easily."

"Sure, it will." Ellie grinned. "He won't like me saying this, but I'm going to say it anyway—my brother likes you, a lot. In fact, I've not seen him as happy with anyone since Lara…and he loved her more than anything."

Marnie's heart skipped a couple of beats. The idea of Joss caring for her in the same way he'd cared for his wife was both thrilling and depressing—because if he did, why would he have said they were done? Done meant *over*, right? Done meant he didn't want her hanging out with his daughters. Done meant he didn't want to see her, touch her, kiss her?

"Thank you for saying that," she said and gave Ellie a swift hug. "But I probably shouldn't talk about him behind his back, considering everything else that's going on."

Ellie hugged her back. "Maybe. But Joss can be stubborn about things—a Culhane trait, I reckon. Anyway, if you need a friend to talk to, give me a call."

Once they parted company, Marnie continued with her shopping. She got home around four, driving past Joss's house and spotting him by his truck in the driveway, the girls standing close by. She noticed how Sissy went to wave when she recognized her car, but the teen's hand quickly dropped. Marnie's heart sank even further and then she caught a glimpse of Joss watching her vehicle. She didn't slow down any more, didn't want to appear as though she was lingering in any way. Back home, she locked herself inside, pulled the drapes together and put her groceries away and was about to make her favorite herbal tea when she heard a knock on her door.

She was certain it was Joss, but when she pulled back the door, she discovered someone else altogether.

Patience Reed.

"I suspect we need to talk," the older woman said through the screen.

Marnie nodded and opened the door and invited her inside. She took her coat and hung it up on the hall stand and then they made their way into the living room. There was a lot of silence in those first, tense few minutes. A lot of long stares, and questions burning on the edge of her tongue. She wanted to know so many things, but she didn't want to push the other woman, either. It would have taken a lot of courage for Patience to come to her door and Marnie didn't want to blow it.

Patience sat on the sofa, her hands in her lap, regarding her intensely. "You know, you look a lot like my sister. She passed away when she was young," she said and sighed.

Marnie's throat closed over. "So, you know… I mean, you accept that I'm your…you know."

"My granddaughter?" She nodded. "Yes, of course."

Marnie exhaled sharply, afraid to think and to want too much from the exchange. "I didn't know you had a sister."

Patience nodded. "What *do* you know?"

She got straight to the point. "I know you gave my mother up for adoption."

"That's correct, I did. I gave up my firstborn," Patience said, her blue eyes glistening a little. "I was seventeen, and I met a boy who was my first love. But when I discovered I was expecting, his parents shuffled him off to relatives in Georgia and I never saw him again. My own parents never gave me the option of keeping her, you understand. I was sent away to a home for unwed mothers for many months before she came. And then, after she was born, she was put up for adoption and I went home."

Patience said it so matter-of-factly, it was as though she'd rehearsed the words in her mind a thousand times but had never found peace in them. Marnie saw the regret in her grandmother's expression and wanted to offer solace, or comfort, or whatever she needed, because she was clearly in pain. But... she had to make sure *her* mother was heard, first and foremost.

"My mother's adoption was closed, so it took a lot of effort to finally find you. Once her adoptive parents were both deceased, she got a lawyer and the case was opened. Then she did eventually have your name, but it wasn't long before she got sick. And she passed away nine months ago."

"I'm sorry," Patience said, her eyes glistening even more. "More than you could know."

Marnie sucked in some air. "I know she wanted to meet you, to ask you what you felt that day, and if you really wanted to keep her. But she died before she had the chance."

Patience winced and nodded. "I wanted to keep her with all my heart," she said, the tears now filling her eyes. "But back then, it wasn't like it is today. Of course, I wish I'd had the courage to stand up to my parents and tell them that I wanted to keep my baby. But it wasn't an option," she said quietly. "A few years later I got married and had my second daughter. But I never forgot the baby I was forced to give up. And I've thought about her every day of my life."

"She thought about you, too."

"Would you tell me what she was like?"

Marnie thought about—considered—whitewashing it and pretending that her mother was happy and fulfilled and lived a life of joy. But that wasn't the case. And enough lies had been told already. So, she quietly and concisely told Patience Reed about the troubled woman her mother had become. She didn't gloss over the hospital stays, the medications, the bouts of mania, the marriage that had been doomed from the start. She didn't make light of the really bad days, when her mom couldn't get out of bed, or go to work, or remember to cook dinner, or do laundry. When she was done, when she was all out of explanations and her chest was hurting so much from the raw emotion being spilled with each word, she let the tears roll down her cheeks.

"But I loved her," Marnie assured the older woman. "Even on the days when it was so very hard."

"I wish I could have been there for you," Patience said and came across the room to sit beside her. "I wish, with all my heart, that I could have helped you."

And then, like she imagined in her dreams, her grandmother took her into her arms and held her, rocking her gently, somehow making up for all of the years and the tears that she'd never seen.

"I'm sorry I didn't tell you who I was when we first met," she said and shuddered. "But coming here—"

"Took courage," Patience said. "And don't ever apologize, Marnie. You have nothing to be sorry for."

She swallowed hard and gripped her grandmother's hand. "But I am sorry if I've made things difficult for you and your family. I mean, with Abby and everyone else."

"Abby is a kind and gentle soul and she'll accept this, and you, without hesitation."

Marnie wasn't so sure. "She was annoyed the other day."

"She was in shock." Patience sighed. "So was I when she arrived on my doorstep Friday afternoon and asked me why you would claim to be my granddaughter."

"And you were forced to tell her about the baby you gave up?" Marnie said, feeling so guilty her heart ached.

Patience tutted. "It was about time it came out, anyway. I'm not ashamed of having had your mother. I never was. It was my own parents who had the shame. And they're now long gone, and they can't make me feel guilty anymore. So, let's not have regrets, okay? Let's work on having a future. I love being a grand-mother to Abby and a great-grandmother to T.J., and I know I'm going to love being your grandmother, too…if that's what you want."

It was, so much. Marnie nodded. "It is."

"So, why don't you pack a bag and come and stay with me for a few days, and we can get to know each other," Patience suggested. "Of course, I know you have to work, but the school is not too far from my house. Unless you think it's too soon?"

Marnie shook her head. "No, I'd like that."

It was settled, and an hour later, Marnie was packed and ready to spend a couple of days with her grandmother. When she arrived at Patience's home, she was unsurprised to find it was a neat three-bedroom bungalow.

"This was Abby's room," she said as they walked down the hall. "Now T.J. uses it when he stays over. Your room is the next one."

Marnie felt a little thrilled. She'd always wanted a place and a room that could be her own with grandparents. Once she was settled, she joined Patience in the kitchen and they sat with coffee and home-baked cookies and talked about everything from her mother, to Cedar River, to local places of interest, and then inevitably, the one subject Marnie wanted to avoid like the plague.

"Well, I heard that you and Joss Culhane are something of an item?"

"Past tense," Marnie said and bit into a cookie. "Very much over."

"You broke things off?"

"He did," she replied. "When he discovered I hadn't told him the truth about why I was in town. Actually, it fizzled out as quickly as it began."

Patience's eyes widened. "But you're in love with him, though?"

"Dreadfully," she admitted and sighed. "Worse luck."

"I've always liked Joss." Patience smiled. "He's such a good father to those girls and God knows being a single parent isn't easy. At one point I'd almost hoped he would catch Abby's eye. But she only ever had eyes for Jake. You, on the other hand…" Patience teased and grinned. "Perhaps you shouldn't give up on love so easily."

She shrugged. "I'm not very successful in the romance department."

"Men find you a little intimidating, I suppose—" her words made Marnie straighten in her seat "—you being so smart and successful. A lot of men can't handle that kind of power imbalance in a relationship. Joss is a successful man in his own right, though… Perhaps that's why he was so drawn to you."

Marnie had no idea why he was *drawn* to her, or anything else. Particularly since he'd dumped her with such little effort. His feelings obviously weren't anywhere near as deep as hers. Hadn't he admitted to being a bed hopper? She should have had more sense than to add herself to his list of conquests.

"I don't think I'll ever know," she said.

"These things have a way of working out," Patience remarked.

"Or not," she said. "Besides, the only relationship that I want to concentrate on right now is yours and mine."

Patience smiled. "I'm proud to call you my granddaughter, Marnie. I hope I can live up to your expectations."

"You already have," she said, emotion clogging her throat.

But she wasn't being as honest as she could have. Because she missed Joss. She missed the girls. She missed him so much it hurt to breathe. She'd only got to love him for a matter of weeks…but they had been the best weeks of her life.

Now she had to get back to the real world, postJoss, and she wondered if she would ever feel truly whole again.

Chapter Twelve

"I don't see why we have to stop being friends with Marnie," Sissy said and glared at him, arms crossed, as they drove to the ranch on Thursday afternoon. "I mean, *we* didn't break up with her or anything."

They had been having the same discussion for close to a week, but Joss wasn't backing down. He had his reasons and they were valid. He'd spent the better part of the week holed up at home or at work, ignoring everything and everyone other than the girls and the workshop. He knew Marnie wasn't at the house, knew she was staying with her grandmother, because Ellie had found out via Abby and she'd then relayed the information to his eldest daughter. Who'd had no hesitation in telling him because she'd made it clear she thought he was a complete idiot for ending the relationship.

Well, he wasn't backing down. She'd screwed up, not him. She'd lied and manipulated and made him believe they were something they weren't. He was the one who looked foolish.

"Because I said so," he replied. "And that's the end of it."

"I can't wait until I'm eighteen and I can do whatever I want," Sissy said heatedly. "And be friends with whoever I want."

"Yeah, at eighteen you can make your own decisions. Until then, I get to decide what's best for you and your sister."

And by then, he thought, Marnie Jackson would be a distant memory for them all.

"You're impossible," she grumbled under her breath.

By the time they got to the ranch, his daughter's temper hadn't abated. He spotted Jake's truck and Hank's police vehicle and figured he should be glad for the company—but he wasn't. He really didn't feel like being sociable. Sissy got out of the car and stormed up to the house and headed directly for the living room, where she promptly ignored everyone and focused on her cell phone. Clare stayed by his side as Joss greeted Mitch in the hallway and rolled his eyes.

"Teenagers," he said on a long breath. "They're so delightful."

Mitch laughed. "Yeah, remember Ellie when she was that age? Oh, they were some interesting times."

"Thankfully, Clare doesn't hate me yet," he said and noticed his youngest daughter had walked on ahead and was now in the living room. "Or maybe she does. So, what's Mrs. B cooking tonight?"

Mitch groaned. "Are you always thinking about your stomach?"

It was better than thinking about anything else, he thought derisively, refusing to remember one single thing about how good it felt to make love to Marnie. He was over it. Done. He had no feelings for her whatsoever. "Yep."

"Ah—Jake and Abby are here," Mitch said and then hesitated. "So is Marnie."

Joss stilled. "What?"

His brother nodded. "She's with them. Patience is here, too."

His gut churned. "Quite the family gathering. I think I'll go."

"Don't you dare," Mitch warned in his best big-brother voice. "Marnie is Abby's cousin—that makes her family. So, whatever is or isn't going on between the two of you, work it out, or get over it."

He wanted to tell his brother to go to hell—but he couldn't and wouldn't. Mitch was the glue that held the family together and Joss respected his brother's patriarchal role. "Okay, point taken. I'll be on my best behavior."

When he entered the kitchen he spotted her immediately, seated next to Abby. It was quite uncanny how alike they were, and he felt stupid for not taking the time to really notice before. Perhaps he would have made the connection and not been so blindsided when he'd found out the truth. She looked up, clearly expecting him, and he managed a tight smile. She did the same and the churning in his gut increased. He wished he smoked or something—so he'd have something to do with his hands.

Mrs. B announced that dinner was nearly ready and suggested everyone take a seat. By now the girls were also in the kitchen and they quickly sidled up beside Marnie and took the seats next to her. He didn't want to think about how that made him feel. Knowing they liked her company and also knowing they'd broken up, he experienced a stupid twinge of betrayal—as though his kids were divided in their loyalty. For years it had only been the three of them, along with his extended family. He was the one who'd brought Marnie into their circle. He'd changed the dynamic. And they clearly needed whatever it was she gave them. Time, he figured. And attention. And kindness and everything he'd always hoped another woman might enrich their lives with.

He was across from her, nowhere near touching distance, but he felt the heat radiating from her as though she were a furnace. He knew it was simply attraction—just lust and desire. But it was strong and had a life force all its own. And stupidly, he resented her for it. It made him feel small and mean. It made him question everything he'd always believed about himself. And then he resented her for that, too. He heard her laugh and the sound polarized him. She looked so comfortable sitting next to her cousin and his daughters—as though she were firmly entrenched into the family.

"Not hungry?"

He barely heard Hank's words. His twin was sitting to his right, grinning broadly. "What?"

"You are so screwed up."

He scowled. "Go to hell."

"Wanna talk about it?" his brother asked. "I'm a good listener."

"I've already had enough brotherly advice from Mitch. I don't need any more."

"Well, I'll be damned," Hank chuckled. "You're in love with her."

"No, I'm not," he denied and felt the lie on his lips.

There was a lot of laughter coming from the other end of the table. He saw there was some activity with Marnie's cell phone and figured there was some kind of video chat going on. The famous cousin, he figured, feeling about as excluded as he ever had from anything. Abby and Ellie and his daughters were all in on the call, and there was more laughter and even some out-of-tune singing.

Of course, he was happy his daughters were having fun. He wasn't that somber or petty. He just wasn't sure he wanted them having fun with Marnie, since he'd made it clear he didn't want her anywhere near them.

After dinner, everyone headed for the living room, except for Joss, who stayed and helped Mrs. B clean up. It was something he'd always done. Except this time, Marnie hung back, too, saying very little as she grabbed a tea towel and began drying glassware too good to go into the dishwasher. When they were done, Mrs. B bade them good-night and disappeared through the back door to head for her cabin behind the main house.

And they were alone.

"I see you and Abby have made amends?" he said.

She nodded. "Patience helped soothe things over."

"Things are good with your grandmother, I take it?"

"Great. She's a wonderful person and I feel very fortunate to have her in my life now."

"Looks like everything has worked out for you, then," he said and tossed the tea towel onto the counter.

She swallowed hard. "Are you still angry with me?"

"What do you think?"

"I think we should talk more," she replied and

sighed. "Look, I'm sorry, okay? I made a mess of things and I should have told you the truth from day one…but honestly, I was a little overwhelmed with being here and starting a new job and dealing with the possibility of meeting my grandmother for the first time. And I know that sounds like an excuse," she said, waving a hand, "but it's all I've got."

"It's not enough," he said, staying on the other side of the counter, because all he really wanted to do was take her in his arms and kiss her like crazy. "I'm just a simple guy who tries to lead a decent life raising my kids and running my business. And all I know is I would never use anyone to get to the end goal."

"It might have looked that way, but it wasn't deliberate."

"Wasn't it?" he shot back. "Are you really going to try and justify it by saying you didn't know, or didn't realize, or didn't think it would matter?" Joss shook his head in disbelief. "Damn it, I let you into my life. I let you into my kids' life. I haven't done that with anyone since Lara died. That's the kicker here, Marnie…my daughters care about you, I see the way they are with you and what they're longing for, hoping for, and knowing you were pretending the whole time is—"

"I care about them, too," she implored, cutting him off. "And I swear that none of it was pretend. Not being with the girls. Not being with you. It was the most real time of my life." She stood on the other side of the counter, breathing hard. "Joss…I'm in love with you."

The air sucked out of his lungs and he stared at her, wanting to believe her so much he could feel his knees weakening, his resolve slipping. But he couldn't believe her. "Do you think that's the answer? Do you think that changes anything?"

"I…hope so."

He shook his head. "It doesn't."

"Haven't you ever made a mistake?" she asked.

He nodded. "Yeah, a few weeks ago I made the biggest mistake of my life."

She winced. "You don't mean that. I know you're not hurtful for the sake of it. I know I made a mistake and I'll own it. But we were in this *thing* together and I know what I felt… I know how you made me feel. And you can deny it, you can stand there and say you don't love me back, but I don't believe it. I think you do love me," she said, her back straightening, looking more beautiful and passionate than he'd ever seen her. "I think you love me and it's scaring you to death. And I think being mad at me for not telling you about my grandmother is just the excuse you need, so you can bail." She inhaled, hands on hips, her gaze pinning him. "Because you're not ready to love someone. You're not ready to give that part of yourself to me or anyone else, because loving someone means you might lose them. Loving someone is risky. And you haven't risked yourself for a long time."

His back straightened. She was pulling him apart, piece by piece. "You don't know anything about it, or me."

"But I do," she said defiantly. "I know you live in your safe little world of one-night stands every second weekend. I know that you love your daughters more than life itself. I know that losing Lara almost broke you in two. I know that you think the accident that injured your brother was your fault. I know that you haven't called your father back because if you do, you might forgive him, and if you forgive him, he might hurt you all over again."

"Marnie," he warned, "stop."

"No," she said. "I won't. Because sometimes people hurt you, even if they don't mean it. And being hurt doesn't end you, it doesn't destroy you… I know that for a fact. I was betrayed by a habitual cheater because I didn't think I deserved any more than that. Yeah, it might feel like it at the time, it might feel like you're going to break into two…but that's not real. It's how we bounce back that counts. How we get up and move on. Like you should do from Lara, from your father." She stopped, taking a breath, giving him a chance to regroup for a second. "You know, Joss, loving someone else doesn't mean you love Lara less. And seeing your father and forgiving him doesn't mean you become like him in any way. It just means you're not hanging on to that anger and rage. It means that you're giving the rest of the world a chance. Giving yourself a chance to be happy. All I know," she said and pressed a hand to her heart, "is that I love you and I want to be with you."

Her words cut at him rawly, deeply. He didn't want her or anyone else speculating about his reasons for not contacting Billie-Jack. He didn't want anyone wondering why he hadn't had a serious relationship since Lara died. He didn't want Marnie getting inside his head and seeing that he was terrified of not measuring up. And he didn't want her saying she loved him.

But she was right. About Billie-Jack. About Lara. And knowing she had his number made him feel more vulnerable and exposed than he ever had in his life. And he knew what he had to say.

"I don't want you to love me," he said flatly.

"Too late."

But he was out the door before he could see the hurt in her eyes.

After four weeks of working at the school, Marnie was in her groove. Her life in general was in a groove, she thought, as she collected the quizzes her students had left on their desks. She had spent a lovely few days with her grandmother and their relationship was getting stronger every day. She had also made amends with Abby and discovered they had a lot in common. Plus, she'd found a good friend in Ellie. She'd even received a text from Joss after that ill-fated evening at the Triple C, saying he'd reconsidered his position and she could spend time with his daughters if that was what they wanted. Nothing about their relationship.

Nothing about forgiving her or loving her.

And really, she was tired of thinking about it, tired of wondering how it all went so spectacularly pear-shaped in such a short time. So, she concentrated on the good things. On Patience. On having another cousin. On the family she now had.

"I wish you'd marry my dad."

It was Clare who said it. Right after class when all the other students had left and Marnie was collecting the quizzes. She looked at her and smiled. "Sometimes things just don't work out."

"I don't understand adults sometimes. You act like you have all the answers, but then you act all stupid about it. Dad said I had to stop saying stuff about it."

"He's probably right," Marnie said gently.

"He's just being stubborn."

"Maybe," she offered. "But I'm sure he thinks he's doing what's best."

"Marrying you would be what's best," Clare said and huffed. "So, would you marry him if he asked you?"

Marnie raised a brow. "He's not going to ask me, so we shouldn't speculate, okay?"

"But if he did," Clare asked again, with extra drama, "would you?"

Marnie couldn't lie. "Yes, I would."

Clare grinned a little. "Then you'd be my mom, right?"

She nodded and shuddered out a breath. "Shouldn't you be waiting outside for your dad to pick you up?"

"Aunt Ellie is picking me up in five minutes," she replied. "Daddy's gone away for a couple of days."

"He has?" she asked, her interest piqued. "Where to?"

Clare shrugged. "He didn't tell us."

Marnie's insides sank. It was a Friday and he'd gone away? Maybe he was seeing someone. Having a vacation. A hot and steamy weekend. Oh, God... she wanted to fall in a heap. And then she wanted to smack herself for being so ridiculous and predictable. She'd offered him her love and he'd rejected her. She didn't need to hear those words again in a hurry.

"You should get going," Marnie said and was startled when Clare rushed forward and gave her a hug.

"I wish you were my mom."

Marnie's heart rolled over. "Oh, honey. I know you do. I wish I could tell you that everything will work out."

Clare swallowed hard. "I think my dad loves you."

Marnie hugged her again. As much as she'd tried to convince herself he didn't care, she couldn't. He wouldn't have pushed her away so harshly if he wasn't invested in her and in them. He just couldn't let himself love her for reasons of his own.

Marnie watched as Clare left, and realized the little girl had taken a piece of her heart with her. When she got home she showered, changed, ate a noodle cup over the sink and watched TV for a while. She was just turning into bed at ten when her cell pinged. It was Joss.

Did you tell my daughter we were getting married?

Marnie laughed out loud and replied quickly.

Of course not. She asked me if I WOULD marry you. I said I would. If you asked.

A message came back a few seconds later.

That's kind of the same thing.

She responded swiftly, smiling a little, which was a nice change from crying all the time.

No, it's not. I said I would. I didn't say you had asked.

Her cell pinged again.

Well, I haven't asked. So, can you stop filling her head with the idea?

She typed out a response and hit Send.

I'm not promising anything. Where are you, by the way?

It didn't take long to get a reply.

What?

Clare said you were out of town. Romantic getaway?

He responded with a grumpy emoji.

Not likely. Personal errand. Good night.

She toyed with her reply and then settled on the truth.

If you want your daughter to stop matchmaking, then maybe you should fall out of love with me.

The grumpy emoji returned. Along with I'm not in love with you.
She replied within seconds.

Sure you are. You're just too chicken to admit it.

He didn't respond. She didn't expect him to. And she hurt so much she could barely breathe.

* * *

Joss wasn't sure what to expect when he met Billie-Jack for the first time in two decades. Of course, he knew the old man was sick. Knew from Grant and Mitch that the illness and treatment had taken its toll. But the small, thin man in front of him wasn't who he remembered. There was a hollowness in his expression and a vacancy in his gaze that conflicted with his memories of the man who had been an abusive drunk, who'd belted him countless times with a strap, who'd rarely said a kind word in those last few years.

What amazed him, though, was in that moment, he felt nothing.

Not anger, not resentment, just indifference.

He had to admit, the old man appeared to have turned his life around. His lady friend, Mindy, was polite and offered him coffee and there was no sign of alcohol or any other kind of excess in the small house.

"Is this your first time in Arkansas?" she asked.

He nodded and turned his attention to his father. "So, why have you been calling me? What do you want?"

Billie-Jack pushed forward in his seat. "You know what."

"Forgiveness?" he queried.

Billie-Jack shrugged. "I'm not after a miracle. I just wanted to see you, to tell you I was sorry for everything that happened."

"For what?" Joss shot back. "For checking out after Mom died? For getting drunk five days out of seven? For almost killing Hank? For bailing because you didn't have the guts to face what you'd done?"

It was a long list of accusations, each one of them true, each one laced with the hurt he'd felt back then, as a fourteen-year-old boy who'd needed guidance and comfort after losing his mother—and instead got belted with a strap. And then the indifference he'd always clung to, the indifference that had somehow kept him from feeling anything, slowly morphed into something else, something he knew he'd suppressed all his adult life—anger.

"You had one job, *Dad*," he said, staying in his seat, even though he was itching to get up. "To look after your kids when they needed you. That's all you had to do. You didn't have to be father of the year, you didn't have to drown your sorrows in a bottle— you just had to step up and look after your kids."

Billie-Jack nodded slowly. "Like you did," he said and linked his bony hands together. "After your wife died."

His throat burned. "Yes, exactly."

His father nodded again. "There's a difference, though. You're strong, like your mom. I wasn't. I was weak and scared. I didn't want to live after your mother died. I didn't want to face life without her. I shut down because I didn't wanna feel anything— because feeling things hurt too much."

Joss stilled, and as his anger slowly dissipated, it was replaced by something else—acknowledgment. *Self-ackowledgment.* Because, in a way, hadn't he done exactly the same thing after Lara had died? He'd shut himself down emotionally, channeling all his energy into raising the girls and work, hiding behind meaningless one-night stands for years and refusing to admit what he was really afraid of—loving someone and then losing them. Like he'd lost his mom. And Lara. And, in a way, Billie-Jack. It was easier—and safer—to shut down, to pretend he had enough to do with being a father and running his business, and that he wasn't so wretchedly lonely most days that he ached inside.

Until Marnie had entered his life.

With her blue eyes and soft voice, she'd turned his emotional switch back on. She made him think, yearn, *feel*…for the first time in forever. But the fact she was in town for only six months had waved like a red flag and, in a way, was the perfect excuse for him to hold back. Learning she hadn't come clean about her identity and her real reason for coming to Cedar River was all he needed to cement that excuse. In the end, it was an easy out.

And one of the hardest things he'd ever done.

All I know is that I love you and I want to be with you.

Her words came back and hit him with stunning clarity, and in that moment he knew exactly what he wanted. And who. It didn't matter that they had known one another only a short time. It didn't matter that she'd felt the need to keep her identity a secret. All he knew, deep in his heart, was that he was in love with her. He had the rest of his life to live, and if he was lucky, he'd live that life with Marnie at his side.

Joss got to his feet and looked at his father. "For a long time I blamed myself for the accident," he said and saw the startled look on Billie-Jack's face.

"You did?" his father asked. "Why? It wasn't your fault."

"It's hard to feel logical at fourteen. I thought that maybe if you and I hadn't got into it that day, you might not have taken off in the truck, drunk. I thought you might have slept it off and the accident might never have happened. But it did happen. *You* were drunk. *You* drove with your kids in the back seat. *You* didn't care about anyone or anything other than yourself. *You* have to live with that. *You* have to learn how to forgive yourself." He took a long breath, finding strength from the air in his lungs. "But I don't need to forgive you. Frankly, I don't need anything from you. What I need isn't in this room. It's back home with my kids and my family, and the woman I love."

He stood and looked at Mindy, then back at his father. "Take care of yourself, Billie-Jack. And I hope you both have a happy life. Goodbye."

With that, he walked out and closed the door.

* * *

Marnie had spent several days in varying emotional states. Happy because she was reconnected with her grandmother and had quickly grown to love the older woman. And heartbroken because she hadn't heard from Joss and suspected that their fledgling relationship was over before it really had a chance to begin. The truth was, she missed him. She missed their talks and their laughter, and she missed his touch so much.

She went to Abby and Jake's on Saturday morning, along with Patience and Ellie, and had a lovely time learning how to make choux pastry. Abby was such a talented chef, and a great teacher, and by midday there were trays of sweets laid out on the kitchen countertop. By one, Mitch and Tess had arrived, and Hank turned up shortly after. Even Grant and Winona, who'd been in newlywed bliss for the past few months, according to Ellie, made an appearance. Everyone was excited about the baby they were expecting, and Tess was already insisting they have the baby shower at the ranch.

Everyone was there. Except for Joss and the girls.

"I'm not sure what's wrong with Joss lately," Jake said, shrugging.

They were on the front deck, enjoying the cool, clear weather, drinking coffee and eating cake after a barbecue lunch, and Marnie knew she was the center of everyone's speculation. Natural, she supposed, that they would all be curious about the state of her relationship with their brother. And really, she felt so at ease with them all, she couldn't do anything other than smile and shrug.

"Beats me," she said and knew everyone could hear. "I just happen to love the guy."

She got a few sympathetic looks and then felt embarrassed to the tips of her hair.

"Isn't that Joss's truck?" Ellie asked and pointed to a vehicle driving toward the house.

"Yep," Hank said and chuckled. "Sure is."

He was back from wherever he had been. Personal errand, he'd called it. She wanted to strangle him for making her wonder if he'd been with another woman. The girls got out first and came racing toward the house. She wondered if any of the family thought it odd that they made a beeline for her first. She didn't have too much time to speculate, though, because within seconds of hugging each girl, his brothers were all laughing loudly.

Because there he was, getting out of his truck, dressed in a *chicken* costume. A giant, feathery, yellow chicken costume with only his face peering out from a round gap at the front. He strode to the bottom step on big red chicken feet and stopped, looking up at her. Only her. And ignoring everyone else.

"What are you doing?" she asked, too stunned to laugh.

He flapped the wings. "Proving to you that you were right… I am chicken."

Her heart soared. "You are?"

He shrugged. "Turns out you were right about a lot of things. So, I figured, if I'm gonna do this, then I do it in front of everyone, and then I'll have no excuses and nothing to hide behind."

Marnie's eyes filled with moisture and as she looked at him, dressed in the ridiculous costume, she'd never loved anyone more, ever, in her entire life. "Okay…do it. I'm listening."

He took a deep breath, glanced at the family she knew he adored and then met her gaze head-on. "I never imagined I would love anyone ever again. I never imagined I'd be lucky enough to find someone that makes me laugh. I never imagined I would find someone who would be so kind and generous with my children. I never imagined I would find someone who saw me for who I am, who knew why I was scared to make a commitment. Or would know why I didn't want to talk to my father after so many years. Which I did, by the way," he added and shrugged again. "Which is where I've been for the last couple of days. We didn't make amends. But he listened."

"And the guilt?" she asked, knowing she was the only person who knew what was in his heart.

"Gone."

"How does it feel?"

He nodded. "Good. Anyway, back to me being—

what did you call me the other night—too chicken. Well, yeah, I have been. But the thing is, I never imagined that I would screw up so badly," he said and shrugged, "and that you would forgive me because, for some reason, you seem to be in love with me."

Marnie inhaled, not bothering to stop the tears in her eyes. "I am in love with you."

"Well, despite how it's probably seemed over the last couple of weeks, I love you, too," he admitted and she heard the girls squealing excitedly beside her and she heard Abby and Patience sniffling a little. "And I want to give you the rest of those things on your bucket list. I want to share the aurora borealis," he said and grinned. "And I want to stroll down Champs-Élysées with you, I want to take you on that gondola ride in Venice, and I want you to have that wedding you've always dreamed about and the babies you want to have. I'll watch soppy chick flicks with you. I'll even listen to old disco music with you, because I know it's your favorite. And despite being a little afraid of heights, if you want to go skydiving, then we'll go."

"You'd do all that for me?"

"I'd do anything for you. And just for the record, I got this costume from a fried chicken outlet in Rapid City. It cost me four hundred dollars and it smells like grease and is really itchy."

She laughed, she laughed so hard she had more

tears in her eyes and then she raced down the stairs and straight into his feathery arms. Which tickled her skin and did smell like grease—but she didn't care. She was his, he was hers. And he kissed her, in front of everyone, he kissed her as though they were the only two people in the world. She heard cheers and knew his family—her family now, too—wholeheartedly approved.

"I love you," he said against her lips. "I'm sorry I said I didn't. I'm sorry I said I didn't want you to love me. I do…and more than that… I need you and your love, like I need air to breathe and the earth beneath my feet."

"You're quite poetic when you want to be," she said and grasped his hand from under the feathers. "And if we're clearing the air, I have a couple of things I'd like to say."

He smiled. "Can I shake off this chicken costume first?"

"Sure," she replied. "Let me help."

She wondered, for a second, what everyone was thinking as they watched from the balcony. But when she turned, she noticed that the balcony was empty and the family had gone inside.

"We must have looked like we needed some alone time," she said and helped him out of the costume.

"That, or they couldn't bear seeing me humiliate myself any further," he said and made a face.

She giggled. "This is all kind of romantic, you know."

"It will be something to tell our kids," he said and laughed.

She touched his face and then removed a few stray feathers from his hair. "Joss, what made you—"

"Come to my senses?"

She nodded a little. "Yeah."

"You. Clare. Sissy. The fact that I've been miserable for the last couple of weeks and have missed you like crazy. But I couldn't deny you were right—I was scared of loving again. Scared of losing, I suppose. Scared of hurting."

"I can't promise not to die," she said and touched his face again. "But being with you is where I want to be for the rest of my life."

"And you were right about Billie-Jack, too," he admitted, linking their hands together. "I've spent so long hating him and blaming him, I think I lost sight of why. And then thinking I was somewhat responsible for the accident… It all kind of got twisted up and I couldn't articulate to myself why I acted like I didn't care, but inside was still so angry after all these years. The fact is, he's old and dying, but even when I was young, I was never that invested in him, you know. I was closer to Mom and when she died I was angry because he didn't step up and fill that gap. I didn't have the relationship with him that Grant did, or even Jake—who fought him the most, but still wanted to have a relationship, I suppose. Because of that, it makes him easier to let go. All I want is to be a better father than he was, and I think I am."

"You are," she assured him. "You're a wonderful dad."

"Thank you. And I promise I will try to be a good husband."

She nodded. "I know that. And, Joss, you do believe that I didn't ever deliberately manipulate you. I know it might have looked that way, but I promise, that was never my intention."

"Of course, I know that. I was angry because I was feeling a whole lot of stuff I couldn't control. I don't blame you for wanting to find your grandmother and I certainly don't blame you for wanting to keep the information private."

"I'm so glad I found her."

"I'm glad you found her," he said. "Because of that, we found each other."

She kissed him gently, softly, and with all the love that was in her heart. They had a wonderful future ahead, which made her the luckiest woman she knew.

And she intended on letting him know that every day for the rest of their lives.

Epilogue

Three days after Joss's dramatic chicken proposal extravaganza, Marnie was still reeling from the fact she had a man who loved her, two kids who were simply wonderful and a whole extended family who had welcomed her with open arms.

She got home from work on Wednesday and there was a note pinned to her door.

My backyard. Six o'clock. Don't be late.

She showered and changed and walked the fifty yards to his house. Her house, too, soon enough, she figured, although they hadn't talked about the specifics of their new life much. When she rounded the driveway she spotted candles dotting the path and she followed them around the back. The gazebo was shimmering with candles and lights and there was a small round table set up with champagne and canapés. And Joss stood by the step, a rose in his hand, wearing a suit and tie and looking so incredibly handsome she turned weak at the knees and knew she'd never tire of admiring him.

The girls were there, too, standing by the steps, their faces beaming with smiles.

"What's this?" she asked when she greeted them.

"Well," he said, reaching for her hand. He drew her into the gazebo and gave her the rose. "A couple of things have occurred to me."

"And what are they?"

"The first thing is that although we've talked about marriage and babies, I never actually got around to proposing."

"Oh, well, I just assumed—"

He dropped to one knee, still grasping her hand, and holding out a small black box. "Marnie—I love you with all my heart and soul. I want to spend the rest of my life with you. Will you marry me?"

He flicked open the box and she saw a bright solitaire diamond flanked by pink stones.

"It's beautiful."

"The girls helped me pick it."

She smiled and looked at both Sissy and Clare. "It's exactly the ring I would have picked out."

Sissy nodded and grinned. "So…you haven't answered Dad's question."

Marnie looked at him and then his daughters in turn and experienced a great surge of love that swelled her heart. "Yes, Joss, I will marry you."

The girls squealed delightedly and both hugged her before he slipped the ring on her finger and got to his feet, kissing her soundly.

"Okay, girls, time for you both to go back to the house," Joss said quietly.

His daughters moaned and then begrudgingly headed up the path, turning every few steps to giggle and nod approvingly.

Then he poured champagne and passed her a glass. "You've made their day," he said. "Mine, too."

Marnie smiled. "And mine."

"When are you going to marry me?" he asked.

"We should probably have a reasonably long engagement," she suggested. "Since we've really only known one another for a short time. I was thinking twelve months?"

"Six," he replied and smiled.

She nodded. "Done."

"I guess you'd like a big wedding, huh?"

She tried to look coy. "Very much. I'd like the girls to be bridesmaids and Shay to be my maid of honor. I'd even like my dad here, to give me away."

He nodded. "How does a wedding at the ranch sound? We can have it outside, under a tent."

"Wonderful. You said a couple of things?" she reminded him.

He cleared his throat. "Well, yeah…so, besides the proposal thing, we haven't talked about what you're going to do when your job contract is up."

She looked at him and laughed. "Darling, I just said yes to your marriage proposal. I'm pretty sure that means I'm staying put in Cedar River."

He sighed with actual relief. "Whew…that's good to hear. Okay, and our living arrangements. I may have made us an appointment to view the house by the river tomorrow…if that's okay with you? I mean, I like this house and I've been happy here, but I think a new place would be good for us. I know the girls would agree. And if we have a couple more kids, we'll need more room."

She almost swooned. A new house. A wedding. Babies. Her life had certainly turned out different than she'd imagined. "I'm okay to look for a new house, as long as I can help pay for it. I have a bit of money saved. More than a bit, really. A lot. But we can split things down the middle. I want us to share everything. You could rent this house instead of selling it…or maybe have it in trust for the girls when they're older. And you're right, a new home, with lots of rooms for the girls and all the babies we're going to have is a great idea. I'd like two, by the way."

He flicked on some music and drew her close. "I'm sure I can manage that."

She shivered, knowing the promise of what was to come. "Dancing, too?"

"You bet, my love."

Marnie smiled. She had everything she'd ever wanted. And more.

* * * * *

Catch up with the previous books in
The Culhanes of Cedar River,
Helen Lacey's miniseries for
Harlequin Special Edition

When You Least Expect It
The Soldier's Secret Son
The Nanny's Family Wish
The Secret Between Them
The Night That Changed Everything

wherever Harlequin books and ebooks are sold.

**WE HOPE YOU ENJOYED
THIS BOOK FROM**

◆ HARLEQUIN

SPECIAL
EDITION

Believe in love. Overcome obstacles. Find happiness.

Relate to finding comfort and strength in the
support of loved ones and enjoy the journey
no matter what life throws your way.

6 NEW BOOKS AVAILABLE EVERY MONTH!

HSEHALO2021

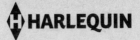

HARLEQUIN

*Uplifting or passionate,
heartfelt or thrilling—
Harlequin has your
happily-ever-after.*

With a wide range of romance series that each
offer new books every month, you are sure to
find the satisfying escape you deserve.

Look for all Harlequin series
new releases on the
last Tuesday of each month
in stores and online!

Harlequin.com

HONSALE0521

COMING NEXT MONTH FROM

⊕ HARLEQUIN
SPECIAL EDITION

#2863 A RANCHER'S TOUCH
Return to the Double C • by Allison Leigh

Rosalind Pastore is starting over: new town, new career, new lease on life. And when she buys a dog grooming business, she gets a new neighbor in gruff rancher Trace Powell. Does giving in to their feelings mean a chance to heal...or will Ros's old life come back to haunt her?

#2864 GRAND-PRIZE COWBOY
Montana Mavericks: The Real Cowboys of Bronco Heights
by Heatherly Bell

Rancher Boone Dalton has felt like an outsider in Bronco Heights ever since his family moved to town. When a prank lands him a makeover with Sofia Sanchez, he's determined to say "Hell no!" Sofia is planning a life beyond Bronco Heights, and she's not looking for a forever cowboy. But what if her heart is telling her Boone might just be The One?

#2865 HER CHRISTMAS FUTURE
The Parent Portal • by Tara Taylor Quinn

Dr. Olivia Wainwright is the accomplished neonatologist she is today because she never wants another parent to feel the loss that she did. Her marriage never recovered, but one night with her ex-husband, Martin, leaves her fighting to save a pregnancy she never thought possible. Can Olivia and Martin heal the past and find family with this unexpected Christmas blessing?

#2866 THE LIGHTS ON KNOCKBRIDGE LANE
Garnet Run • by Roan Parrish

Raising a family was always Adam Mills' dream, although solo parenting and moving back to tiny Garnet Run certainly were not. Adam is doing his best to give his daughter the life she deserves—including accepting help from their new, reclusive neighbor Wes Mobray to fulfill her Christmas wish...

#2867 A CHILD'S CHRISTMAS WISH
Home to Oak Hollow • by Makenna Lee

Eric McKnight's only priority is his disabled daughter's happiness. Her temporary nanny, Jenny Winslet, is eager to help make Lilly's Christmas wishes come true. She'll even teach grinchy Eric how to do the season right! It isn't long before visions of family dance in Eric's head. But when Jenny leaves them for New York City... there's still one Christmas wish he has yet to fulfill.

#2868 RECIPE FOR A HOMECOMING
The Stirling Ranch • by Sabrina York

To heal from her abusive marriage, Veronica James returns to her grandmother's bookshop. But she has to steel her heart against the charms of her first love, rancher Mark Stirling. He's never stopped longing for a second chance with the girl who got away—but when their "friends with benefits" deal reveals emotions that run deep, Mark is determined to convince Veronica that they're the perfect blend.

YOU CAN FIND MORE INFORMATION ON UPCOMING HARLEQUIN TITLES, FREE EXCERPTS AND MORE AT HARLEQUIN.COM.

HSECNM0921

SPECIAL EXCERPT FROM

H HARLEQUIN
SPECIAL EDITION

*Raising a family was always Adam Mills' dream,
although solo parenting and moving back to tiny
Garnet Run certainly were not. Adam is doing his best
to give his daughter the life she deserves—including
accepting help from their new, reclusive neighbor
Wes Mobray to fulfill her Christmas wish...*

Read on for a sneak peek at
The Lights on Knockbridge Lane,
*the next book in the Garnet Run series and
Roan Parrish's Harlequin Special Edition debut!*

Adam and Wes looked at each other and Adam felt like
Wes could see right through him.

"You don't have to," Adam said. "I just... I accidentally
promised Gus the biggest Christmas light display in the
world and, uh..."

Every time he said it out loud, it sounded more
unrealistic than the last.

Wes raised an eyebrow but said nothing. He kept
looking at Adam like there was a mystery he was trying
to solve.

"Wes!" Gus' voice sounded more distant. "Can I touch
this snake?"

"Oh god, I'm sorry," Adam said. Then the words
registered, and panic ripped through him. "Wait, snake?"

"She's not poisonous. Don't worry."

That was actually not what Adam's reaction had been in response to, but he made himself nod calmly.

"Good, good."

"Are you coming in, or…?"

"Oh, nah, I'll just wait here," Adam said extremely casually. "Don't mind me. Yep. Fresh air. I'll just… Uh-huh, here's great."

Wes smiled for the first time and it was like nothing Adam had ever seen.

His face lit with tender humor, eyes crinkling at the corners and full lips parting to reveal charmingly crooked teeth. Damn, he was beautiful.

"Wes, Wes!" Gus ran up behind him and skidded to a halt inches before she would've slammed into him. "Can I?"

"You can touch her while I get the ladder," Wes said.

Gus turned to Adam.

"Daddy, do you wanna touch the snake? She's so cool."

Adam's skin crawled.

"Nope, you go ahead."

Don't miss
The Lights on Knockbridge Lane
by Roan Parrish, available October 2021 wherever Harlequin Special Edition books and ebooks are sold.

Harlequin.com

Copyright © 2021 by Roan Parrish

Get 4 FREE REWARDS!

We'll send you 2 FREE Books plus 2 FREE Mystery Gifts.

Harlequin Special Edition books relate to finding comfort and strength in the support of loved ones and enjoying the journey no matter what life throws your way.

FREE Value Over **$20**

YES! Please send me 2 FREE Harlequin Special Edition novels and my 2 FREE gifts (gifts are worth about $10 retail). After receiving them, if I don't wish to receive any more books, I can return the shipping statement marked "cancel." If I don't cancel, I will receive 6 brand-new novels every month and be billed just $4.99 per book in the U.S. or $5.74 per book in Canada. That's a savings of at least 12% off the cover price! It's quite a bargain! Shipping and handling is just 50¢ per book in the U.S. and $1.25 per book in Canada.* I understand that accepting the 2 free books and gifts places me under no obligation to buy anything. I can always return a shipment and cancel at any time. The free books and gifts are mine to keep no matter what I decide.

235/335 HDN GNMP

Name (please print)

Address   Apt. #

City   State/Province   Zip/Postal Code

Email: Please check this box ☐ if you would like to receive newsletters and promotional emails from Harlequin Enterprises ULC and its affiliates. You can unsubscribe anytime.

Mail to the **Harlequin Reader Service:**
IN U.S.A.: P.O. Box 1341, Buffalo, NY 14240-8531
IN CANADA: P.O. Box 603, Fort Erie, Ontario L2A 5X3

Want to try 2 free books from another series! Call 1-800-873-8635 or visit www.ReaderService.com.

*Terms and prices subject to change without notice. Prices do not include sales taxes, which will be charged (if applicable) based on your state or country of residence. Canadian residents will be charged applicable taxes. Offer not valid in Quebec. This offer is limited to one order per household. Books received may not be as shown. Not valid for current subscribers to Harlequin Special Edition books. All orders subject to approval. Credit or debit balances in a customer's account(s) may be offset by any other outstanding balance owed by or to the customer. Please allow 4 to 6 weeks for delivery. Offer available while quantities last.

Your Privacy—Your information is being collected by Harlequin Enterprises ULC, operating as Harlequin Reader Service. For a complete summary of the information we collect, how we use this information and to whom it is disclosed, please visit our privacy notice located at corporate.harlequin.com/privacy-notice. From time to time we may also exchange your personal information with reputable third parties. If you wish to opt out of this sharing of your personal information, please visit readerservice.com/consumerschoice or call 1-800-873-8635. **Notice to California Residents**—Under California law, you have specific rights to control and access your data. For more information on these rights and how to exercise them, visit corporate.harlequin.com/california-privacy.

HSE21R2

Don't miss the next book in the Wild River series by _USA TODAY_ bestselling author

JENNIFER SNOW

In the Alaskan wilderness, love blooms in unlikely places—and between an unlikely couple...

"An exciting contemporary series debut with a wildly unique Alaskan setting." —_Kirkus Reviews_ on _An Alaskan Christmas_

Order your copy today!

HQNBooks.com

PHJSBPA1021

Love Harlequin romance?

DISCOVER.

Be the first to find out about promotions, news and exclusive content!

Facebook.com/HarlequinBooks

Twitter.com/HarlequinBooks

Instagram.com/HarlequinBooks

Pinterest.com/HarlequinBooks

YouTube.com/HarlequinBooks

ReaderService.com

EXPLORE.

Sign up for the Harlequin e-newsletter and download a free book from any series at **TryHarlequin.com**

CONNECT.

Join our Harlequin community to share your thoughts and connect with other romance readers!
Facebook.com/groups/HarlequinConnection

HSOCIAL2021